Metaphorosis

March 2020

Beautifully made speculative fiction

Also from Metaphorosis

Metaphorosis Books

Reading 5X5 x2: Duets
Score – an SFF symphony
Reading 5X5: Readers' Edition
Reading 5X5: Writers' Edition

Metaphorosis Magazine

Metaphorosis: Best of 20xx
Metaphorosis 20xx: The Complete Stories
annual issues, from 2016

Monthly issues

Plant Based Press

Best Vegan Science Fiction & Fantasy
annual issues, from 2016

from B. Morris Allen:
Susurrus
Allenthology: Volume I
Tocsin: and other stories
Start with Stones: collected stories
Metaphorosis: a collection of stories

Metaphorosis

March 2020

edited by
B. Morris Allen

ISSN: 2573-136X (online)
ISBN: 978-1-64076-165-0 (e-book)
ISBN: 978-1-64076-166-7 (paperback)

Metaphorosis
a magazine of speculative fiction
from
Metaphorosis Publishing

Neskowin

March 2020

The Eighth Fathom

Chris Panatier

First Fathom, The Plunge
In a past beyond the reach of time's measure, we fell from the Galaxy Beam and into the waters of a primordial world. From the shattered wreckage of our Great Hull, we salvaged the ascension core and dove into the salted darkness. And within the abyssal contours of this alien planet, we made our home, awaiting the wobble of the zenith star that would presage the Beam's return.

Ook crept down the leg of the ocean platform, moving her arms slowly over its metal surface so her suckers might taste its various alloys. She descended at a starfish pace, careful not to flood her mantle too quickly or jet water through her siphon too forcefully. Any unnatural vibration could give away her presence to the other octopuses below. That would be unacceptable—Ook was, after all, a spy.

Technically, she was a low-level scout, sent to monitor the far reaches of her den's territory. But now that she'd actually spotted someone, an adjustment of title seemed due. Casting herself in a blotchy rust pattern, she continued through the murky water until her keen eyes made out the situation—the gathering of octopuses pressed in against the base of the giant leg, intent on some task. *What is the logic of this?* Ook wondered. Slinking forward, she could see two of their number tending to a knot of wires protruding from the leg while the others watched. Hopefully they wouldn't look up or she'd be done for.

A medium sized Bimac held the bundle while another, a tiny Mimic, delicately unspooled the tangle and plucked a few wires from it. The observers then split their ranks to allow passage for a colossal Great Pacific tugging a heavy cable behind. The Mimic expertly spliced the wires to the Pacific's heavy cable and then retreated into the circle of onlookers. The Pacific held the opposite end of the cable aloft. From her perch, Ook was able to make out a tool of some kind affixed to the tip. Human in its manufacture and obviously scavenged by this bunch, it had a place for gripping and a long tube that tapered at the end. The circle of octopuses widened.

A great spark lit from the tool's point, searing her retinas. She faltered, stunned, but her arms, having independent neural bundles, tightened their latch. She blinked away the afterimage and tried to process what she'd seen. *What was it, this sun's glint?* She searched her mind for a practical explanation but knew deep down that there was none. Only one thing could have produced the flash, and the big Pacific had it.

The fire that binds. The Seven Fathoms told of it. Though her rational mind resisted the idea, the three hearts within her mantle pounded in primal recognition. *The flame that burns in the water.* Ook widened her aperture, and the water passing over her gills tasted like the breath of truth.

The group upon whom she spied were of a rival den. Known as *Tellers*, they believed in the Seven Fathoms—a spoken history of octopuskind, outlawed as myth by Ook's own den, the *Cephlists*. Ever since hatchlinghood, she had been taught that the Tellers would be the downfall of the species, spreading the Fathoms' lie that octopuses were not of the Earth, filling impressionable brains with the false promise of grand destiny. To speak the Fathoms within the Cephlists' den was akin to heresy; to proselytize them, a death sentence. These prohibitions, though, had not stopped Ook, who had long ago committed them to memory, piecing together the verses from a thousand treasonous whispers. For an octopus of the Cephlists' den, the Fathoms had been her daydream escape from a rigid way of life, but also an aspiration of hope for something vast and wonderful that transcended petty boundaries and ideological squabbling. The light in the Giant Pacific's arm changed everything. The Tellers possessed the fire that the Fathoms foretold. The Fathoms...were true.

An unexpected current caressed Ook's skin. From above appeared the blurry shadow of a human diver in his false shell. Her eyes flicked downward. The

Tellers hadn't seen. The man descended slowly, stopping here and there to examine the platform's various juts and fixtures. If he saw the splice, he would sever it from the cable and the fire would be lost. The thought put a hollow feeling in her cecum. What was there to do? Letting herself be known to the Tellers, much less helping them, was out of the question.

The diver continued down. Ook maneuvered just beyond his reach as her conscience called out, imploring her to act. *You have seen the fire; the Fathoms are true.* Her hearts thrummed. He would see the Tellers any second. *The fire will be lost.* Unbidden, her aperture opened, flooding her mantle as the decision was made. Her head taut with water, she wished a quiet goodbye—a farewell to her den, and to her life—then surrendered to the will that bubbled up.

She blasted her siphon and split the water like a marlin, striking the human on the side of his head. A spray of bubbles exploded from his mask as she sealed herself across his face.

They sank. The Tellers scattered. The man struggled. His gloved fingers scraped at Ook's flesh. They pounded into the seafloor in a cloud of silt. The human drew a short blade and severed one of Ook's arms just above the smallest suckers. Pain strobed over her skin in waves of yellow-white and she inked the water.

Above them, an eight-spoked umbrella of limbs belonging to the Great Pacific appeared. It descended onto the human's head, flashing blue to orange: *confusion.* A quick flurry of its arms asked of Ook a question, *Why are you here, Cephlist?*

Still grappling, Ook made her skin seafoam green—*peace*, an offer of truce while they dealt with the diver. The Pacific crawled to the human's dorsal side and used his chitinous beak to clip a hose, releasing a jet of gas. Ook twisted the mask until it filled with water. The Pacific detached and slid away. Ook released as well. The human scrambled upward, his fins beating the water like a shark-bit halibut.

Second Fathom, The Gift

An epoch came and went. We changed, evolved to our adopted world, preserved our tellings. Then, from the shadows of land, bloomed the human era of mechanization, and with it a vessel of steel sent starward. Part of this steel fell to the surface, a great cylinder, equipped on its end with the machinery of propulsion. Curiosities were piqued, but few spoke of hope, for the Gift was damaged. And so we watched the heavens for another.

Ook matched her skin to the seafloor and swept her arms into a high collar about her mantle. Sediment washed side to side in the pendulum current. When it settled out, she found herself walled in by Tellers, poised on hind arms and flashing the red-orange of violence.

She straightened, turned purple-blue in submission, and held up four of her front arms, bending the third down to grasp the tip of a rear arm that passed under her beak.

\|i/

Friendship.

The big Pacific stalked forward, angry colors pulsing his radii. A curt flourish. *I ask again: why are you here?*

Ook swiveled defensively as she considered her answer. They'd tear her apart if she fled—they might tear her apart anyway. She tucked her wounded arm—the one cut by the diver—close and braced herself as she signed. *Please, I am only a scout.*

No! he responded, *You are a spy.* The circle of Tellers shook in outrage. The Pacific signaled them to settle and they obeyed. *Why did you attack the human?*

Ook tightened the corset of arms as if to quiet her hearts' insistent rhythm. All she could think about was the blinding arc of light the cable had produced. Trying to sign slowly so as not to provoke, she answered, *You have the fire that binds, the flame that burns in the water. The Seven Fathoms must be true. The humans cannot know.*

The Tellers' colors altered, arms flashing yellow to green-blue at the tips as they gyred with anxiety. Darkened mantles and emphatic gestures told of violent intentions for the intruder who knew their secret. They urged interrogation, torture, death. Ook nuzzled further into the nest of her arms and blanched white.

The Pacific thumped his arms at once to the seabed, producing a brief eight-pointed puff of silt. *Stop this.* The others calmed, and he came closer, though not near enough to strike. Even outside his capture radius, Ook shriveled some more.

What are you called? he demanded.

She poked the tip of an arm from its coil and drew her sigil. *Ook.*

You will accompany us to the reef.

She released a siphon squirt. A reprieve, even if brief, had been granted.

The Pacific gave some instructions to the others, and they rushed back to the platform to reinforce and conceal the splice. Turning to Ook, he gave his name. *Allops.*

With the splice secured, they headed out from the platform, towing along the loose end of the cable. This was the reason so many had come. They'd had to pull the thick cable's terminal end all the way from their reef, so that once the splice was repaired, they could test that it worked. It did, but now they had to drag it back. A small contingent traveled ahead to ensure clear passage.

Ook had no way of knowing where the Tellers' reef was; scouts sent by her den were leery of venturing too far from their territory. The platform marked the outer limit of her own explorations. She pondered briefly if her den would come for her and concluded, logically, that they would not. As with the not insubstantial numbers who often failed to return, they would assume she'd been eaten by moray or shark. It was liberating, in a way. The Tellers would have no use for the fire that binds if they did not also possess the Gifts. And if they were melding the Gifts with fire, it could only be because they needed a housing for the ascension core. Ook wanted to see it.

Conjuring visions of how it all might be, exuberant blotches scrolled her skin until an acid glare from Allops snapped her to whalesbelly grey. As they marched away from the familiar, she settled her mind within the verses of the Seven Fathoms. *In a past far beyond the reach of time's measure...*

Third Fathom, The Era of Barnacles

Another Gift went upward, carried as if upon a meteor's fire, until the fire died, and the Gift, as with the first, fell. Taste deemed it a prize of great value, a hollow tube forged of delicious and tensile alloys, worthy of the vacuum of space and resistant to velocity. A possible housing, if remade, for the ascension core. A Great Hull to deliver us. But time corroded its potential, for we had no way to shape it. Barnacles spiked and studded its frame. Others still fell, the waste of humankind's drive to break the grasp of their planet. And we languished, unable to bring form to their jetsam.

They drew the cable over the seabed toward the Tellers' reef. Behind Allops and just ahead of a tiny female called Granel, Ook did her best to keep up the torturous pace, but her wounded arm made it difficult. Trying to keep her mind off the pain, she let it wander as they marched. Logic told that if they had the fire that binds, they must then be using it, and while the fabrication of experimental structures might be of interest to an octopus, any effort not devoted to the Great Hull would be frivolous, a novelty— and Ook knew octopuses were too serious for that. She hoped for the chance to gaze upon the Gifts before she was killed, and even imagined being allowed to live, and to brood her eggs in the emanations of their glory.

Ook glanced back toward Granel, who flashed red and made her arm into a hook. *Face forward.* Ook shaded purple-blue, the appropriate response.

They came to rest and Allops instructed them to forage. Famished, Ook scanned the seabed for eye stalks. She fell upon a crab, immobilized it in her arms, and cracked open its head with her chitinous beak. She devoured quickly, and a satisfying heaviness moved to the stomachs in her crown. She used her tongue-like radula to scrape any remnant flesh.

A short distance away, Granel calmly pulverized a large shrimp as she kept watch. Ook freed an arm from around her meal and commented, *Easy food here.*

Granel blinked red-orange, changed to seafoam, and tapped an arm tip into the silt. *Yes.*

Buoyed by the wisp of rapport, Ook fought the urge to probe further. Instead, she gently displayed a modest Yellow Tang, *curiosity.* Maybe Granel would feel compelled to know the source of Ook's inquisitorial hue and start talking.

Granel captured and devoured another prawn. Ook played at the empty crab shell so as to seem distracted, though her pastel flush intensified.

What is it? Granel finally asked, flicking away a shrimps' head in a gesture of annoyance.

You are taking electricity from the platform, said Ook.

Yes. I am aware you saw that.

Fuel for the fire that binds?

Obviously.

Ook hesitated, working up the courage to ask her next question. She inflated her mantle and slowly exhaled through her siphon. *So you can meld and shape the Gifts to form the Great Hull?*

Granel dug into the sand for a scallop and savored it before responding. Ook worried that her inquiry had gone too far, that a captured octopus who couldn't mind her own business wouldn't be worth keeping alive. Granel siphoned from the silt and made for the others. Part way there, she twirled to face Ook and tapped a braid of her forward arms to the skin at her brow. *Of course, what else would it be for?*

Ook's skin burst a joyous Malawi pink before she got control and settled into a tranquil seaweed tone.

Back underway, however, the reality of her predicament began to crystalize. She'd understood the consequences of her attack upon the human, but it had all happened in the space of seconds. Now she felt the weight of her decision. Even if she managed to avoid execution by the Tellers, she could never return to her den. Balarem, the Cephlist chieftain, would assume she'd heard the Fathoms while in the Tellers' custody and have her exiled or sacrificed so as not to pollute purer minds. Little did he know that she'd already imprinted the apocryphal verses and sullied what few friends she could trust with their poetry. Her den's regime was oppressive, but it was still all that she knew. Only that morning—it felt a lifetime ago—she'd crunched snails alongside a dozen of her siblings. The pang of loss would be especially sharp for her fellow scouts: Glodex, Eet, Acil, Teuthis, Lele, Oidia.

The waters darkened and Allops gave word that they would nest down for the night. As Ook waited for sleep, she found herself nursing the fantasy of traveling within the Great Hull as it soared for the Galaxy Beam. She indulged the idea momentarily before spiraling her arms tight to snuff it out.

Fourth Fathom, The Fire that Binds

> Years passed, the verses of our story budding
> and wilting like bulbs on a sea oak.
> Humankind encroached, probing the seabed
> for its lifeblood—the bones of the planet's
> prior masters liquified to black. Upon the
> crests of ocean waves, they raised palaces to
> coax it out, spilling enough to sour the water.
> Their presence brought new gifts to our realm
> —raw materials to which we might apply the
> knowledge of our kind. Piquant alloyed steels,
> levered tools, and machinery of every type gilt
> the sediment. Among them, the fire that
> binds, the flame that burns in the water. The
> spark to meld the Gifts that will carry our
> tellings to the stars.

At dawn, Allops led with new urgency until they arrived at a stunted ridge of coral. The group scaled it and disappeared over the top. Ook followed.

On the other side, a sprawling coral reef formed the skin of a gorge that squeezed to a ravine far below. Granel gave Ook a shove, and she realized that in all of her wonder she'd come to a halt. Descending farther, Ook got her bearings and took notice of the reef's state. Its upper echelons were mottled grays and browns, blunted and crumbling. Branches of coral disintegrated with the mildest caress and the sour-chalk taste of decay clogged her suckers, conjuring in her mind the sad portents of the Fifth Fathom. Near the seabed, the coral regained its polychromatic luster.

A colossal tube lay on the ocean floor, dented, with only small patches of its shiny skin showing through a crust of limpets. Ook recognized it immediately. The steel that had fallen from the sky. The Gift. The holy object that sanctified the Fathoms' words! Right in front of her! She rejoiced that her faith had been confirmed. Further in, more Gifts, dozens of long metal tubes, were set about on short scaffoldings as if being staged for assembly. With so many collected, Ook imagined they could return home with the entire species. Light-mantledness blunted her rapture. She'd forgotten to breathe.

They proceeded deeper into the reef. Ook wore a bland, algae green, hoping not to be noticed by the entire den all at once. They climbed to an outcropping overlooking the ravine. Beckoning Ook alongside, Allops crawled to the edge and cycled his skin red to yellow. *Attention.*

A crowd formed below, with every manner of octopus, from Cirrata to

Smoothskins, Megalels, Mims, and Pacireds, all jockeying for the best spots. Allops swayed his arms in concert with the changing patterns of his skin, and the jittering crowd fell still.

I have returned from the source, he declared. *I have restored the fire that binds.* Ook glanced nervously to Granel, who flashed yellow-green-blue before smothering it. Meanwhile, the multitudes made their skins as bright as Pink Dorids —gratitude for Allops' achievement.

And, he paused, allowing the suspense to build, *a human attacked us in his false shell!* The crowd's saturated pink warmed to the hues of awe and wonder. *I attacked and repelled him before the splice was discovered.*

Yellow and orange seeped into the onlooker's mantles. Excitement, adoration. Ook felt her skin pushing to red in the face of Allops' lie, but suppressed it.

That is not all, he continued, *I captured a spy.*

His words sent the crowd gyring and flashing colors of surprise, anger, and violence. Ook wedged herself into a cubby and patterned her skin after the reef, mimicking the coral's parenchymal texture. Her camouflage was for naught, as all eyes were already attuned to the outsider. She was afraid now, but felt no regret for the decision that had put her there.

Allops reached into the nook and uprooted her. She resisted instinctively, twining her arms around his and squirming, trying for a bite. The much larger Pacific easily shrugged away her attacks. *The thing about spies,* he said, holding her wriggling body aloft, *is that eventually they get caught.* A thick arm snaked around Ook's mantle.

Allops constricted, crushing her aperture, and she quickly exhausted herself in a futile struggle with the giant's grip. Stagnant water bathed her gills. Images faded to a mist of shadows and she fell limp. As twilight closed in, she triggered her ink sac, but with her mantle paralyzed, only a dribble darkened the water. At least, thought Ook, she'd seen proof of the Gift before the embrace of death. The Fathoms—upon whose verses she'd built her dreams—seemed to be true. And as she suffocated, the emotion that cut through the black was happiness.

A buffeting current found her in the aphotic dusk of semi-consciousness.

Ook's mantle came free and inflated, pulling water across her starving gills. A tunnel of sight returned in time for her to see Allops, with Granel latched to his mantle, sinking into the stunned crowd below. They hit the seabed in a twisting knot of arms. Allops fought to pry the much smaller octopus away, but his defenses quickly became lethargic and passive. Granel kept hold until he stopped moving, then released and siphoned back to the outcrop.

Ook lay where she was, arms sweeping in the current, as the horizon of her own demise receded. Granel peeked from the underside of a thick trunk of coral, flashed Tang yellow, and tapped the point of an arm into the meat of another. *Are you okay?*

What happened? asked Ook with much effort. *Is Allops dead?*

He may die. But he is large.

It was then that Ook took notice of Granel's markings. She'd not paid attention before, as dens tended to be poly-species. Her glowing aquamarine ring pattern meant she was *Lunulata*. Just about all octopuses had venom. A Blue Ring's was the most potent.

Did you...bite him? asked Ook.

Yes.

Ook's skin cycled blue-orange. *Why?*

You saved the fire that binds. You are a useful octopus.

If he is not killed, said Ook, refreshing her mantle, *he will come for you.*

Perhaps, said Granel with a casual swish of an arm. *Let us find >\|||/<.*

>\|||/<? asked Ook.

The Teller.

Fifth Fathom, The Poisonous Wake

Humankind conquered the salt, and from their bow wave we fled. Finless, they became lords of the water, taking first the surface and next the floor, infecting all with the excrement of their industry. Left awash in their poisonous wake, the breath of our world turned acid within our mantles. And the zenith star wobbled in our burning eyes.

Ook kept close to Granel as they slithered through the congregation, its members now cloaked in the soft Molly Fish-yellow of cautious inquisition. Allops lay amongst them, his eyes blindly open, mantle inflating and deflating anemically. Ook doubted the movement would supply his gills with sufficient oxygen. She hoped not.

The crowd quickly thinned. A dead or dying octopus was hardly a rare thing, after all, and Ook understood that Allops' death would be met with a sort of indifference. Ever conscious of their short lifespans, octopuses were not a species that mourned. The only reason they'd lingered at all had been the spectacle.

Ook followed Granel through a narrow channel. Around a bend, it opened into a wide bowl formed from the reef itself. A flash of magnesium-white lit the perimeter. Spooked, Ook darted under a burl of coral.

Granel peeked in. *The fire that binds,* she reminded her.

Ook crawled from her spot and squinted. Around the circle were even more of the giant steel tubes, where workers used fire in bursts to meld and form them. Their work strobed the coral, painting her vision in colors vibrant enough to taste. To her octopus's eyes, it was a disorienting spectrum of emotional hues. She focused on the sand.

Granel led her by an arm to the center where a ring of adolescents had formed around a centuries-smooth stone. On top sat a Giant Pacific munching a conch. Ook had never seen an octopus eat conch, as the shells were too hard and thick for even the strongest beak. The magnificent animal let the broken shell tumble from the stone and settled into a weave of crimson arms. He blew a jet from his siphon and cast his squat pupils over the young, then cycled his colors and launched into the Seven Fathoms. This was >\|||/<, the Teller.

For Ook, witnessing the Fathoms told all at once rather than as smuggled fragments, was like seeing the sky for the first time. That they were recited—or rather, *declared*—openly, anointed them with majesty, and she felt buoyed upon their swelling truths. ...*a vessel of steel sent starward...upon the crests of ocean waves...when the Galaxy Beam makes perigee.*

When the Teller finished, the others dispersed and the big cephalopod reversed the spiral of his arms. He shifted an eye. *Is there not work to be done?* he asked of the lingering pair.

Ook slid behind Granel and matched her pattern.

>\|||/<'s eyes followed her. *I know what you did, little octopus,* he said. *You saved the splice.*

Ook managed to curve an arm tip out from under herself. *How do you know?*

Octopuses, he said, *eating up gossip like razor clams.*

Granel scooted forward. *I am concerned about Ook's safety here.*

After what you did to Allops? His big mantle rumbled in a way that was something like a chuckle. *I struggle to believe any octopus will be foolish enough to come for the tiny spy just to fall dead by your venom.* He looked Ook up and down. *You are not large, but you will be of help in the builders' ring.* He opened his aperture wide and took a deep inhalation before sending a cloud of silt outward with a siphon blast. They'd been dismissed.

Sixth Fathom, The Verse of Sepias, The One Who Escaped

Soon came our introduction to the curiosity of humankind, with its inquiring fingers probing our living flesh as it would a seabed or the virgin sky. Sepias was a captive, who after losing two arms to curiosity's blade, fled, living just long enough to give of his learnings. The humans blundered upon an ancient string of our code that leads them to question our origin. Now, we must make the Beam before they learn we are their betters, before they do as humans do.

Over the next weeks, Ook concluded that she was not going to be killed by the Tellers. Some even expressed their gratitude once they'd learned the true story of her heroics in preserving the splice. Nothing more was seen of Allops.

Ook did what she could to help the builders at their jobs. Due to her size, this amounted to handling small tools or dragging bits of steel from one place to another. She relished the work, taking the opportunity to run her suckers over every material, savoring each new taste as she went. Massive sections were completed, bundled, bound by fire, and set aside.

The launch of the Great Hull was set to coincide with the den's reproductive season. Granel confided to Ook that she had already accepted sperm packets some months earlier from a submissive Blue Ring called Flen, and had laid her eggs shortly after their return from the platform. When she wasn't completing her own small tasks, she could be found tending to them in a ravine-side cranny.

One morning, Ook and Granel went about the builders' ring resupplying each station with narrow rods of the tangy alloy they used for melding. Ook had dropped off several armfuls and was headed back to the staging area for more when the lights flickered. The builders made themselves blue-orange as their fires blinked out. The coral, once screaming with color, faded into the background, a sunken shade of twilight dust. All eyes flowed to the Teller's stone. >\||/< spoke the words they were all afraid to say. *The splice.*

Granel flew to him and puffed herself big. *The humans have found it! Ook and I will journey to the platform and conduct repairs. I know the splice.*

The Teller scanned the circle. *What of Flune and Autilus?* he asked, referencing the same octopuses Ook had seen mending the splice on the day she was captured.

Hunting, answered Granel.

>\||/< glanced at Ook, who signaled her eagerness to help. *Very well,* he said. *You may lead the way. Take with you*

some builders for safety. Make haste. The cable is our salvation.

They conscripted five builders—all Great Pacifics—and traveled the channels toward the outskirts of the den, then up the face of the reef along the cable. They swept over the top, then ran as fast as their arms would take them, adding siphon jets whenever they had the breath.

Not far from the reef's boundary, Granel dropped into the sediment and flashed to camouflage. Ook followed suit, burrowing up to her eyes. The others held back, disguised, but too large to bury themselves. Ahead, a biogenous fog hung ominously above the seafloor. *What do you sense?* asked Ook.

Motion, answered Granel.

An army emerged. The Cephlists—what had to be every member of Ook's den—charged through the veil of debris. Flashing red, arms bearing blades of shell and shattered coral, they came for the Tellers' den. Ook flattened herself further. There was only one reason her people would have ventured so far from their territory: to put an end to the Fathoms, to stomp them out once and for all. The cable had led them straight to the reef.

The builders raced for home. Ook deployed her ink and siphoned in retreat. To her surprise, Granel did not follow, rising instead from her spot to face the angry throng. Ook cycled her colors in alarm and gesticulated for Granel to flee. Instead, the diminutive Blue Ring turned seafoam and fanned her arms in the way of friendship.

\|i/

And she was cut to pieces.

Ook's hearts plummeted like anchors into the abyssopelagic and her color drained as she stood from her hole, disbelieving. One of the Great Pacifics pulled her backward in retreat.

They fled. Ook blew jet after jet until her eyes clouded from oxygen deprivation. She darted up the reef's edge, bound her arms, descended its slope like a torpedo, and shot through the ravine while broadcasting the colors of danger. She came to the circle and skirted the Great Hull. Halfway up the reef, she found >\||/< attempting to direct the builders in the almost-darkness.

My den has come, exclaimed Ook. *Granel—*

The cable.

Yes. They followed it.

Warn as many as you can, said the Teller, pulsing black to red. *Order them to retreat here.*

I will.

Ook scurried into every channel, warning those she found, imploring them to do the same. Word spread riptide fast and soon the entire reef was lit in alarm.

The Cephlists swarmed the lip of the gorge, a murderous wave, sweeping over its contours like sheets of sargassum, wiping out Tellers too slow to escape. In the ravine below, Ook and the others scrambled for anything they might use to defend themselves—bits of alloyed scrap or shards of coral broken from the stalk. A great number of the attackers Ook recognized—some, of course, were her siblings.

Just shy of the builder's ring, Ook found a wedge of steel and passed it into the arm she believed would make the quickest strike. She retreated to the Teller's Stone where >\||/< remained, unarmed. From the ground near one of the Gifts, she collected a bundle of shanks and swam boldly into his capture radius, offering them up.

No, he said.

You must defend yourself.

>\|||/<'s arms swept into motion, *I need no defending.* And for some reason, Ook took him at his word, though she couldn't think why. A new fervor punctuated his gestures, the accent of his signs striking her in some deep, atavistic place. The boldness of his declaration seemed to elevate him above the coming death as if he were inoculated against it, and Ook thought she detected an auric halo about his mantle. *Call them close,* he said.

Ook kept hold of her steel and siphoned to the perimeter, where she hurriedly encouraged others into the circle. The ring around the Teller's Stone swelled in numbers, as frightened octopuses packed together. The first wave of Cephlists emerged from the reef's capillaries just behind, their apertures rimmed lava red, weapons glimmering like sardines.

They slowed as they bled into the open, apprehensive of potential traps. The Tellers, unprepared and outnumbered, had gone white with terror, a tacit admission that they'd failed to fortify the reef. Ook, who like all octopuses had always understood the fleeting nature of cephalopod life, wanted to live now more than ever before. The other Tellers must have felt the same, otherwise they would have risked their lives to fight the invaders. But none did. Even in the face of slaughter, they held out for a miracle so they might live to ascend.

The invaders wreathed the Tellers like stalking moray. There would be a signal, perhaps, or an act of violence that would trigger a final cascade to wipe them all out. Ook watched, barely cycling her water, anxious to see which it would be, and curious as to who would come for her. She readied herself, hearts pounding. Tension built like magma below an abyssal vent.

And then their arms fell limp. Weapons dropped. Red-orange mantles cycled to violet, the color of awe. Their eyes traced upward, to something behind Ook. She twisted to see and found herself bathed in a soft, silver light.

>\|||/<'s head was glowing. His eyes and beak showed as shadows against the light burning from within, making for a

terrifying, wondrous, sight. The face of death, thought Ook, if there was such a thing.

He siphoned from the stone and loomed above them. *Behold,* he said, *the artifact, the relic of our time before the Plunge, the proof, protected and kept by the Tellers across an era that split the crust, hidden from the predations of humankind. Its radiance now tells that the ascension is nigh, for the Galaxy Beam has arrived.*

Arms whispered through the reef, speaking recognition for what >\||/< had concealed within his mantle. Ook felt it too, and something within her code communed with those around her. She felt enveloped by the collective understanding that they were all descendants of the Plunge, and a sense of fellowship embraced and warmed their many hearts.

Except for one.

A Cephlist hovered up from the crowd, his arms spread wide, weapons gleaming from the curl of each tip. Ook froze mid-breath, aperture agape. The octopus blasted his siphon and made for >\||/<. The Teller lashed out, and then the attacker was sinking, his many blades sparkling down like shattered abalone. Curious, Ook swam to the fallen aggressor. No others paid any mind, still mesmerized by the Teller's luminous head and the ascension core within it.

She curled up beside the dying octopus and saw that it was Balarem, the Cephlist chieftain. The impact of >\||/<'s strike had crushed his gills, and his mantle spasmed to force enough water over them. He wouldn't last long. She looped an arm underneath his head. Casting herself blue-orange, she asked, *Why would you attack now? You can see by the Teller's glow that the Fathoms are true.*

He struggled for a breath, then answered, *That the Fathoms could be true is why they were forbidden.*

I don't understand. Why?

He shuddered as his mantle flickered white-yellow. Then his arms whispered an answer that speared Ook's hearts and sent the limbs of her mind aquake.

Discombobulated, uncontrollable waves of hot red-orange strobed her skin as she struggled to form a response. Finally, she whipped a retort. *There is no way to prove what you say.*

Balarem's aperture flopped open and his eyes went distant. With the tip of an arm, he said, *And there is no way to disprove it. Which is why…the Hull…can never ascend.*

That can't be right! Ook raged. *We have seen the wobble of the zenith star! We have the core! The Beam has come! No, no, no!* She squeezed and caressed the dying octopus so that he might revive and be convinced of the absurdity of his postulate. When he didn't, she sped away, leaving him to drift on the seabed.

Seventh Fathom, The Great Hull

> Upon our mastery of the fire that binds, and upon the gathering of as many gifts as could construct the Great Hull ten times over, we will assemble a vessel formed of the artifacts of Earth, then select those among us who will leave it. They will be pure of mind, unsullied by life. The Great Hull with its lading shall be host to the ascension core when the Galaxy Beam makes perigee. Only then may it rise.

>\|||/<'s ebullient mantle intensified over the following days. While no one knew what form the Galaxy Beam would take, >\|||/< hypothesized it to be a great technology, something like a squid's

tentacle that reached from one galaxy and into another, both transporting settlers and snatching them back up years later. The ascension core was a complementary piece, detecting the signature of the Beam's approach, and then latching to it when in close enough proximity. The changing light in the Teller's head seemed to bolster his theory.

The cable—cut not by humans at all, but by the Cephlists before the attack—was repaired, and a tremendous effort brought construction of the Great Hull to a close. It took the full strength of both dens—thousands of arms pulling—to bring it upright. Modeled after the form of their kind, it had a colossal central tower surrounded by eight smaller ones, with enough room for scores to travel. Ook basked in its magnificence, making Balarem's objections seem small and short-sighted by comparison; paranoid musings of a zealot newly aware that he could no longer bend the world to his narrow view of it. Ook pressed any thought of him from her segmented mind.

It only remained to be decided who would be chosen to make the journey home. With the final preparations complete, >\||/< took to the Teller's stone. He draped his arms like a sea star as the denizens of the reef gathered. Ook, planted nearby and twitching with excitement, tried not to ink.

>\||/< pulsed red-yellow, casting the reef in amber radiance, and began. *When the first Teller took the ascension core within his mantle, he understood that he would not be the one to carry the Great Hull aloft. Nor would the millions of Tellers since the first. It was passed down as a trivial rite, a burden no larger than a moon jelly. To those early Tellers, the arrival of the Galaxy Beam was a distant apparition, an event they would never live to see. Now it is here, and the charge of carrying the core to the stars has fallen to me.*

Understanding his meaning, the question was asked, *Who will ascend at your side?*

>\||/< blew the stone clear of sediment and responded, *No one.*

The reef burst red. *You cannot do this! You lied to us! We built the Great Hull! We have a right to go!* Many jostled for the Hull itself.

Ook watched the chaos, too stunned by >\||/<'s revelation to join in the madness.

Think of what you ask! he said, then waited for their fervor to dwindle. *Ascension to the Beam is an act of suicide.*

They went still.

The cold of space will freeze the Great Hull and the water inside to a block of ice within minutes, he continued. *Anyone within will perish.*

A pearl-blue Megalel siphoned up from the mob. *The ascension core will protect us!* she declared. A nearby contingent cheered her optimism.

Don't be fools, >\|||/< answered. *There is no evidence it will do any such thing. Even if the Great Hull could support life, this journey will be measured by the cycles of planets and stars, not by the span of one, or even a million of our lifetimes.*

Why did you let us build such a large structure if your plan was to ascend alone?

It was the only way to ensure that the Great Hull was built at all—every Teller had to believe they might to be chosen for the ascension.

The octopuses allowed their arms to murmur their displeasure, but they recognized that the Teller's logic was sound. *What, then?* was the question asked.

>\||/<'s mantle became brighter. *We will send to our progenitors the story of our time here. A telling of our survival and evolution. And they will know in the sending that we wish for communion.*

Who will deliver the telling? they asked. *How can it be done if none can survive the journey?*

We will send our eggs.

It was like the ocean currents had reversed. The dictates of the Seventh, and final, Fathom, suddenly took on new meaning. Its directive, that those chosen for the voyage home would be *unsullied by life*—what Ook had always considered an embellished call for those pure of heart—had been meant literally.

Clutches had only just begun to be laid, said one. Another, flashing red and yellow, announced, *What eggs we had were destroyed in the attack! We need time to spawn new broods.*

There is no more time, said the Teller.

Ook raced from the assembly. Hearts thundering, she counted the inlets along the ravine until she came to a tiny cave. Inside, on a thick trunk of coral, hung a ribbon of milky teardrops. Leaning close, she tapped one and a reef's worth of tiny eyespots swiveled to the vibration. She went to work, carefully detaching the clutch from its anchor point. As she completed her task, Balarem's warning slithered again through her neural bundles. She paused only briefly, determined to continue on the course she'd chosen, and finished collecting the eggs.

>\||/< slid from his rock when he saw the parcel nestled in Ook's arms.

They are the octopus Granel's, she said, presenting them. *Lunulata.*

The Teller took them softly, saying, *Her sacrifice will be remembered then, as her code will be our telling.* He twisted for the Great Hull. *It is time.*

The light of >\||/<'s mantle was blinding as he made for the vessel, and Ook understood his intention to ascend at that very moment. Her dreams had always painted this moment as an event of great joy and fanfare. >\||/<, though, said nothing, made no grand pronouncements or gestures. He slid into a small chamber at the base of the Hull, and the few remaining builders used fire to seal him inside.

The Great Hull lifted from the silt, light as a jelly. Its metal skin quavered, then took on the sheen of sunset on sand.

Acicular crystals appeared—small at first—but growing long like the spines of a great sea urchin. And as she watched, Ook's mind perceived something that other animals would recognize as *sound*—for octopuses cannot hear. She did not know that what she perceived was music—a rising symphony that hummed through her stomachs and carried her hearts on the wings of its soaring melody. And with it came a thrilling clarity that coursed from her mantle into her arms, to the brim of every sucker. For a speck of time, she touched home...or maybe it was home that had reached out to touch her. She felt *seen*, recognized—included in the order of whatever she was. Then the music ceased, and she was just Ook again.

The crystals studding the Hull stretched long and golden as it made for the surface. The reef's inhabitants swam alongside, well-wishers in a vertical procession. Ook sprinted ahead. The Hull broke the waves and continued steadily into the air, pulled on an invisible tether toward its destination far above. As it pierced through a feathering of clouds, the crystals slid away and sliced into the water.

Others breached, and together they watched until the Great Hull was a dot, and then until the dot was no more. Before sinking back down, Ook surveyed the horizon, the platform in the distance, and wondered how long it would take for the toxifying ocean to crawl up its legs. The threads of an idea knit through her arms as she stared, weaving together and taking shape in her central mind. And it was then she saw clearly the course of her species on Earth. It was time to speak.

Below, the only evidence that the Great Hull had ever existed was the copse of towering crystals spiking the sediment, their tips aspiring skyward. The octopuses returned to the reef, skins draped in gray, stoic. No one spoke or flashed. None rejoiced. The Great Hull had taken with it their purpose, leaving them to wash in a listless current. The Seven Fathoms, once the guide to their future, had become the past.

Ook, blue-green and unsure, crawled to the top of the Teller's stone. She knew the implication well enough. To occupy the stone was to declare oneself the Teller. Others shuffled forward, drawn by her audacity and curious to see what she would say. Her arms, unthinking, danced the choreography they'd always ached to give, as she delivered the Fathoms openly and without fear of expulsion or death. At the conclusion of the Seventh Fathom, she paused to refresh her water. And then, for the first time, she offered a new verse.

Eighth Fathom, The Postulate

And so it was, that before we sent the Great Hull aloft, the octopus called Ook held in her arms the saboteur Balarem, who spoke as he died of an alternative telling. And he allowed in the last inflations of his mantle, the true reason the Cephlists had condemned the Fathoms. *They do not tell us why we fell.* And in the glow of the Teller's mantle, the postulate was laid. That the reason for leaving our home, for unclasping from the Beam, had been to escape it.

The reef was frozen in shock. Many turned white, some red. In their millions of years on the planet, the Fathoms had been an unambiguous call to home, toward which the Tellers had devoted their existence. Now the Eighth Fathom offered a haunting new perspective on the

First: the Plunge as successful escape rather than tragic accident. In launching the Great Hull now, so it went, they'd signaled their presence and undone themselves.

The crowd gyred its distress. Why had Ook not reported the saboteur's words before the ascent?

The new Teller, \|i/, who had once been the octopus Ook, considered their questions. Changing her color to gray-indigo, she pinwheeled her arms to tranquility posture. *The ocean swirls with poison,* she said. *The humans, too, will someday complete their learning and come for us. What lives at the distant end of the Beam may be our salvation, and the clutch of eggs borne of the octopus Granel is our entreaty. We could not risk missing the chance to commune with them.*

But what if the entreaty fails? the others asked. *What will become of us?*

Even if what we have summoned brings death, it cannot harm us if we are already extinct. We will begin the second octave of our time here, said the Teller. *And prepare for the new Gift.*

A new Gift? Their colors were Tang and blue-green. *What is it?*

It is the rising sea, said \|i/.

Hues of confusion rippled through them.

Soon the water will reclaim the land, she said. *As man fled the shores and despoiled our seas, so upon a surge of their own making shall we swim into their dens.*

For what purpose?

Who here wishes to drift idle in the slack tide while the progeny of Granel make way for the place of our origin? We did not fall from the Beam to languish. We will journey into this new territory, make ourselves known. Survive.

Understanding, the octopuses of the reef cycled azure and dispersed. There were eggs to lay, shellfish to hunt, preparations to begin.

\|i/ slid from the Teller's stone and tapped a contingent of Great Pacifics to go with her to the platform, where she would place a mark upon one of its legs. Set an eel's length above the surface, it would serve to trigger their migration when the deepening waters finally swallowed it. With the cable as their guide, they embarked from the reef.

The trajectory of their species, she realized, had forked like a branching coral. Its fledgling limbs were the divergent paths of \|i/ on Earth, and the children of Granel who charged the void. For a short distance along the seabed, she allowed herself the daydream of their descendants reunited in some future millennium, and began spinning a verse that would preserve the memory of Granel's great deeds. Then her mind turned to the trials ahead, and the Eight Fathoms dimmed like sunbeams through the mesopelagic.

*See Chris Panatier's story "The Eighth Fathom"
online at Metaphorosis.
If you liked it, leave a comment. Authors love
that!
Remember to subscribe to our e-mail updates so
you'll know when new stories are posted.*

About the story

I am a huge science fan, and so find myself reading any number of articles that I half understand. A year or so back, there was a rash of reports dealing with cephalopod DNA/RNA and how much of it seems to fall outside the typical evolutionary scheme for Earth-based animals. My natural conclusion was, "Well, look at them. They're obviously aliens." Many sideline commentators have made the same remark, most of the time only half-joking.

What is undisputed is that cephalopods, and octopuses specifically, are highly intelligent. They can solve puzzles, use tools, recognize faces—the list goes on and on.

Pair these two features of the octopus with the fact that human beings have been dumping used stage one rocket boosters into the ocean for over half a century and the story sort of writes itself. Highly intelligent, marooned octopus explorers are finally given the tools to build themselves a ship and return home. That's an oversimplification, but that was the very first kernel for what became "The Eighth Fathom."

I learned an incredible amount about these creatures and really fell in love with them. At the same time, the story addresses the role humans are playing in the destruction of ocean habitat, and the interesting response of these particular octopus dens.

A question for the author

Q: Are you optimistic about the future of humanity?

A: Depends from whose perspective the question is asked, doesn't it? From my perspective, no. And I'm an optimist. And while I have a generally positive attitude about *humans,* I do not hold out much hope for the species as a whole, if that makes sense. MLK said that the arc of the moral universe is long, but it bends toward justice. We make strides here and there. Socially, moreso in the past fifteen years than the many years prior. This is a good thing. But not if we commit suicide via climate change. It's already happening.

The problem, as far as I can see it, is the consolidation of power and control around the world in a handful of people who are not good; who for short term financial and political gain, unwind environmental protections, burn rain forests, dump poison and trash into the oceans and water table, and then deregulate the industries that pollute. Greed, and the fear of shrinking fortunes by those who have them, are perhaps the most potent driving forces behind the failure of humankind to do something about the crisis.

From the perspective of a future nature that doesn't include humans, I'm very optimistic.

About the author

Chris lives in Dallas, Texas, with his wife, daughter, a herd of dogs, and possibly one goat. He also does album art for metal bands, and generally employs his borderline ADD to any number of projects at the same time. He is also a civil trial lawyer representing people who have been poisoned by negligent corporations.

www.chrispanatier.com, @chrisjpanatier

The Wicked Stepmother

Rhema Sayers

She was five when I married Reynard, a sweet, shy child, bewildered by the loss of her mother. At first, she rejected me. But with patience and understanding, a gentle approach, and a lot of stuffed animals (the first 20 or so went out her tower window), I was able to help her overcome her grief and anger. For years we grew steadily closer. She became my daughter. Then when she was thirteen, she changed, almost overnight. I seriously considered having Father Friedrich attempt an exorcism. The idea still crosses my mind occasionally.

Every day was a battle: arguments, screaming, foul language. She wanted to go to parties, but wouldn't tell me where or with whom, snarling that it was none of my business. She wanted to go to sleepovers at a friend's, but never knew the friend's last name. When she was fifteen, she wanted to be able to drink wine. Several of her classmates were going to Anvelkan on the coast for spring break, and she wanted to go. Alone. No security. Of course, the answer was usually no, and I was always the one to hand down the decision. Reynard was too busy being Reynard II, King of Vesla and Emperor of the Golden Isles.

She was the Crown Princess, schooled in court etiquette and protocol, yet she saw no problem appearing in public wearing almost invisible bikinis. And the makeup! She looked like she'd been learning from Fast Freda, the whore who has the corner at Market and 5th.

Dinnertime was particularly stressful, since Reynard insisted that she eat with us.

"How was school today, Snowy?" I asked one evening.

Reynard put his fork down and, shaking his head, covered his eyes.

Snowy glanced up at me under long, dark lashes, her bright blue eyes flashing with anger. She tossed back her long black hair.

"Fine," she grunted.

"Did you learn anything interesting?"

"No."

"What are you studying now in history?"

She grimaced. "Can't we just eat dinner?"

"I was just trying to learn about your day, dear."

"Stop prying into my affairs!" she exploded. "What do you care anyway? You hate me just like you hated my mother!"

I reeled back. "I don't hate you. I love you, Snowy. And I never knew your mother."

"You're trying to take her place! You're not my mother! You're just a horrible old witch! I hate you!" she screamed and threw down her fork, spraying Lobster Newburg across the pristine white tablecloth. She bolted, knocking over her chair.

I stared at my plate, appetite gone. "Horrible old witch?" I whined.

Reynard stretched his hand out toward me, although the table was too long for him to reach. "You take this too personally. She doesn't mean it. And you're not old." Love and concern warmed his voice, although I had trouble seeing him past the candelabra.

I glared at him "So does that mean I'm a horrible witch? And what way am I supposed to take it?"

"Well, Elizabeth says we should loosen up our restrictions on her. Give her more of a free rein. She thinks…"

"Elizabeth is a meddling idiot." I snapped and I, too, exited…hopefully with more dignity.

Reynard keeps saying that it's a phase, that she'll grow out of it. Reynard is a great King, but he's useless when it comes to his daughter.

My Ladies-in-Waiting agreed with Reynard, and with Elizabeth, the Prime Minister. Lady Marta told me about her daughter, Lizette, how horrible she was. "And now we're just the best of friends," she simpered. But Snowy's anger and resentment of me were escalating. I thought something more was going on. Someone was actively turning her against me.

I was tired of having Elizabeth, Lady Bywaters, Duchess of Kurness, Reynard's

Prime Minister, butt her rather long nose into our personal affairs. She never liked me. She nearly had a hemorrhage, when Reynard started dating me and fairly bled to death when we got married. She didn't like commoners, especially commoners that married kings. I remember how she looked at me when we first met. The hate that sparked in her dark blue eyes lasted only a moment. If I hadn't been watching, I would have missed it. My maids told me that she had been making moves on Reynard. Apparently Prime Minister wasn't good enough. She wanted to be the Queen. Reynard seemed oblivious to it all.

Two nights ago, the guards had caught Snowy sneaking out the postern gate at the back of the vegetable garden. I grounded her indefinitely. Furious, she refused to eat or to work with her tutors. She called her math teacher a... an unprintable word. Madame von Gutsberg resigned. That was it. I had to do something. I sent for Murdoch. I know. I know. Murdoch is a thief and an assassin, but he was my guardian from the time I was three, and I trust him. I assigned him to watch her.

Grounded or not, she got out again.

"She's meeting a boy named Harold, son of Seymour the Sly, the new chief of the Assassins' Guild." Murdoch was sitting in an armchair in my office, one leg hooked over the arm of the chair, sipping from a glass of red wine.

Shocked, I said "New chief of the Assassins' Guild? What happened to Samvar the Elder?"

"He was pushed off a roof two months ago."

"Why am I finding out about this now?" I asked quietly, temper flaring.

Murdoch looked surprised. "You haven't called me for a report in six months."

I rose and glared at him. "I am the Queen of Vesla! Did it not occur to you that I might be interested in any changes in the organized crime hierarchy?" Then I stopped and thought about it. I reseated myself. He was right. I had been so busy that I had forgotten how valuable a resource Murdoch is. Or how valuable a friend. But I could kick myself later.

"Sorry. You're right. Fill me in."

He regarded me with a raised eyebrow. "You do the Queen thing very well, Genie."

"Don't use that name, Murdoch. No one knows who I used to be and let's keep it that way, shall we? Now what happened to Samvar and where did this Seymour come from?"

Later that night I decided to consult the Mirror. I had found it several years ago in my explorations of the less well traveled portions of the castle. The obnoxious thing usually just says I'm the fairest of them all, as if that were somehow meaningful. It also tends to be extremely sarcastic. Sometimes, though, I can get useful information out of it.

"Mirror, mirror that I see,
What does Snowy want of me?"

A face formed in the glass, green eyes very like mine. "That's a pathetic attempt at rhyme, Regina."

"Yeah, yeah. If you didn't require the poetic intro every time, I wouldn't have to make up ridiculous rhymes. But what is she up to?"

The emerald eyes narrowed, regarding me closely. "You won't like it." the Mirror warned.

"I know I won't like it," I growled. "Just tell me."

"Well, don't say I didn't warn you." A pause for effect. "It appears that she's trying to have you assassinated."

I stepped back, banged into the chair behind me, and sat down abruptly. "She's what?" I squeaked.

"Trying to have you killed. As in dead, defunct, deceased, lifeless, late..."

"But... but why?" I asked, my heart sinking.

"Because she thinks you were responsible for her mother's death."

"But that's ridiculous! I didn't even *know* her mother!" I could feel tears start up.

"You married her husband."

"But... but I didn't even meet him until Giselle had been dead for a year. And that was accidental. He fell off his stupid horse right in front of me and I kept the beast from trampling him."

"I know that. You know that. But apparently Snow White doesn't accept that version of events. Someone is exerting influence over her."

"Who? What can I do?" I wailed.

"You've already had your questions answered tonight. In addition, you'd probably start on another series of 'buts', and I have a headache. Another night and another rhyme. Make it a better one next time." With that, the Mirror darkened and the interview was over.

I couldn't tell Reynard about this development. He doted on his daughter. He wouldn't believe that his little girl could be a vindictive, bloodthirsty little monster. Our marriage hadn't been perfect, but it had been loving and happy. I wasn't willing to upset the status quo by revealing the truth about my past. At least not yet.

As I contemplated this thought, I was walking back to my suite down a dark hallway in the mostly unused part of the castle. Sconces were supposed to light the way, but quite a few were out. I was thinking that I'd have to tell Alfred, the seneschal of the castle, about it in the morning, when three shapes emerged from the shadows and reached for me.

Old habits never die. I smashed the candle into one hairy face, catching his beard on fire. Whirling, I wrenched my arm from the grasp of another and kicked the third in the crotch. The previously silent halls resounded to the screams and moans of my attackers. Beard Guy put out the flames, and he and his uninjured buddy drew blades. They approached with more caution, but with vindictive grins on their ugly faces.

I grinned back at them and that predatory smile made them hesitate. "I wouldn't do this, if I were you," I warned. They laughed, and, together, they jumped me. But I wasn't there anymore. I had pirouetted sideways, and they hit the wall. Kicking Beard Guy in the butt made him lose his balance, crashing to the floor and leaving me just one opponent for the moment. I drew my own knife and pounced on him, slicing his right arm, then dancing away. He screeched and dropped his blade. The moaner on the floor was getting to his feet again, so I had to end this quickly. I slammed my fist into his temple, and he went back down. Beard Guy was back on his feet and I tried kicking him where it would hurt, but the damned skirts interfered and I hit his thigh. He sliced the air an inch from my nose and I dove under his arm and stuck my knife in his side. He howled.

The third one had come up behind me, and I felt a sudden pain in my right arm. Leaving my dagger in the bearded one, I slammed my left elbow into the bulbous nose of my last attacker. He howled, dropping his knife and clapping both hands to his face as blood spurted. I gathered up my damn skirts and ran. They didn't follow.

Back at the residence, I entered through the secret passageway I used when I consulted the Mirror. My Ladies-in-Waiting had their rooms just down the hall from my suite. Sometimes I didn't want them watching me. Changing out of my bloodied dress, I examined the wound in my arm. It wasn't bad, so I washed and bandaged it.

I mulled over this new development. Next time Seymour might send better talent. But I couldn't let anyone know about the attack. Or could I?

Combing my hair, my eyes met those in the mirror, just reflections this time. But the green had gone hard. It was time for a little stepmother-stepdaughter heart-to-heart chat.

I used another secret passageway to get to Snow White's rooms. Pausing at the hidden entrance, which was wide open, I listened. All was quiet except for low murmuring from the sitting room. I slipped into the bedroom. Crossing on the soft blue carpet, I was silent. Snowy and a teenaged boy were half sitting, half lying on a white couch, busily pawing one another.

"Ahem!" I announced my presence.

Two pairs of eyes swung toward me, but they were so tangled up in each other that their noses banged together and they drew back with gasps of pain. I had trouble not laughing.

"Regina!" Snow White yelped. "But you should be...I mean...what are you doing here?"

The boy was on his feet, sidling towards the secret entrance. He was tall and lanky with greasy brown hair falling over his eyes, probably to hide the pimples.

"You! Harold! Sit!" I commanded, pointing at him. And he sat. "Good boy."

I returned my attention to Snowy. "Your three incompetent thugs were unable to dispatch one solitary woman."

Snowy went as pale as her name, and her big blue eyes got even bigger.

My glare skewered Harold. "Tell Seymour to get better talent. And tell him that if he does send anyone else, I won't just hurt them. I'll kill them, and then I'll come and remove his toes with a butter knife. *Capiche?*"

Harold nodded vigorously.

"And as for you, you get your skinny, young ass out of this castle and keep it out, or it will end up decorating the wall in the deepest dungeon...forever. Do...you...understand?" The volume of my voice had risen. I was leaning over him, my nose one inch from his.

Harold nodded and slipped out of the chair from under my looming presence. Continuing to nod enthusiastically, he raced through the bedroom and out the secret passageway.

I sighed. "What good does it do to have a secret passageway, if you tell people about it?"

Snowy had recovered her attitude, rising from her chair. "Why didn't you just kill him? Just bring your guards in and have him thrown out a tower? You can make him disappear. Just like you killed my mother." She was right in my face, yelling.

I had tried to remain cool, but enough was enough. I lost it. I placed my hands on her shoulders and pushed her up against the wall. Staring into her suddenly widened eyes, I snarled "Get this straight, daughter. I don't need guards to make someone disappear. And I didn't kill your mother. I never met her. I don't know who planted this idea in your head, but by all that's holy, I'm going to find out. And then I'm going to make him regret his birth. And understand this." I loosened my hold on her, still staring into her eyes. "I love you, Snowy, and always have. But you're making it difficult." I turned and left, feeling Snowy's gimlet eye drilling into my back, until the secret panel closed behind me.

The next morning, Snow White didn't appear at breakfast. I didn't think His Royal Majesty, Reynard the Second, noticed. He kept his nose buried in reports and only replied in monosyllabic grunts to my comments. Vesla was the site of the annual economic conference for the Five Kingdoms this week. Reynard would be hosting the conference. He was up to his ears in economic forecasts and spreadsheets.

He said, "Check her room. She's probably there, sulking." So much for not noticing.

I went to Snowy's rooms. Lady Gertrude told me her bed had not been slept in. Damn! The girl was out and running around again. I sent word to Murdoch.

He was stymied. None of his sources had heard anything. We talked about possibilities, while Murdoch drank my wine, draped over the armchair. I paced the huge room.

There was a knock, and Reynard came in. He stopped abruptly, when he saw Murdoch, sprawled in the chair. "Hello," he said hesitantly, his perpetually smiling face reflecting some confusion. "Do I know you?"

Murdoch stood up and bowed to his king, making a very nice flourish with his feathered hat. Murdoch is a very handsome man, now in his late forties, always impeccably groomed in the latest styles. "No, Your Majesty. I have never been important enough to come to your attention," trying to look humble and not succeeding. "I am Murdoch, the thief."

Reynard's smile faltered even further, almost slipping all the way off his gentle face. "Oh," he said and looked to me.

"Your Majesty, may I present Murdoch the Agile, the most talented thief in Vesla." I hesitated. But it was past time to come clean. "And the man who raised me when my parents were murdered."

My husband continued to look bewildered for a moment. Then he seemed to stand taller, and the King looked out from his suddenly stern face. "Why have I never met this gentleman, Regina?"

"Because he's a thief, Your Majesty. He tries to keep to a low profile. And we try to keep you separated from thieves and assassins, my liege."

Reynard had never been exposed to the elements from my past. I had managed to beguile him with a tale of an orphan, whose merchant parents had been lost at sea and who had been raised in the church orphanage.

Reynard stared at me for a long minute, his gray eyes suddenly hardening. I began to fidget. "So. Are you telling me that the story of your childhood is just that...a story?"

I stared back at him, weighing my options. I sighed. "Yes, Your Majesty."

Murdoch was carefully levering himself out of the chair. Without taking his gaze from my face, Reynard snapped, "You stay where you are, Murdoch!" Murdoch sighed and sat down.

"Would you care to explain, Regina?" It wasn't a request. It was a command.

I straightened up and looked him in the eye. "My parents were members of the Assassins' Guild. They were very well trained, very talented, but they were killed during a power struggle within the Guild, when I was three. Murdoch saved my life and took me in, when he was just a teenager. I grew up in the Guild and was trained as a thief and assassin. And the only reason Murdoch is the best thief in Vesla now is because I'm retired."

Reynard's eyebrows drew together. "Regina," he said. "A short form of that name could be Genie. Couldn't it?"

I continued to meet his gaze. "Yes, it could."

"And nothing has been heard of Genie for many years."

"She retired to take up another profession."

He nodded. Reynard, like the fox for which he is named, is very quick. "I see."

I regarded him with concern. "Do you?"

Walking to the windows, he looked out over the sunlit roofs of his capital. "I do wish you had trusted me enough to tell me the truth." For a long moment he studied the beautiful scene of orange and red roofs and towers and then he turned back and regarded me. "I love you, woman. The only disturbing aspect of this information is that I was unaware of it until now. I could have used your knowledge. You should have told me!" And for the first time since I wrestled a horse away from his prone body, I saw real anger in his eyes.

Taking a great interest in the colorful mosaic tile floor, I murmured an apology, feeling forlorn, as well as really, truly stupid. "You're right, Reynard. I... I don't have any excuse except...for stupidity."

Murdoch had risen again from his chair and was slithering toward the door. "Sit, Murdoch!" Reynard and I said, almost in unison. We looked at each other and grinned. Murdoch sat down in the armchair, muttering something about things not being fair.

Reynard stepped over to my desk and planted a hip on it, regarding Murdoch with intense interest. "We will discuss this further, Regina. So. Master Murdoch. Just what brings you to the castle this fine morning?"

Murdoch looked to me.

I sighed. "Well, since you're here, you can help us decide what to do, my liege. We have a problem."

He raised his eyebrows. "Problem?"

"Snowy. She's disappeared."

Murdoch chipped in. "And none of my sources have heard any rumors."

Reynard's eyes widened and he paled. "Good God! Why? What happened?" He looked at me. "Did something happen between the two of you?"

I told him about the events of the night before.

"It was stupid of me to be so aggressive, but I was angry." My eyes filled with tears. "I've driven her away! Now she'll never listen to me."

Reynard enfolded me in his arms. "We'll get her back, darling." he soothed. "I'll have Colonel Gebhart start investigating…"

"No!" I yelped. "No! Gebhart's a competent officer, but he knows nothing about the underworld in Heimar. Not like Murdoch and I do."

"What do you suggest?"

Murdoch leaned forward. "Genie and I will go undercover to find her."

Reynard stared at him, then at me, then at Murdoch again. "The two of you? Just the two of you?" He glowered at Murdoch. "You're seriously suggesting that a thief and the Queen of Vesla should go sneaking off in the night in disguise to rescue the Crown Princess from some underworld baron?"

Murdoch frowned. "Well...yes."

"That's...that's preposterous!" Reynard's pallor had changed to ruddy.

I stepped in. "There's no one better qualified. And there's no one else who can carry this off successfully. We'll do it tonight." I turned away and began to pace again while Reynard was still sputtering. "I have a meeting with the wives of the heads of state this afternoon. I mustn't miss that. And there's the welcoming banquet tonight. But I'll get everything organized before then and we can leave right afterward."

Reynard's face was a battleground of conflicting emotions. "Regina. Please. I can't lose you. And while Genie's reputation is formidable, there's much that is unbelievable. There must be another way."

Now it was my turn to turn a stony gaze on my love. "Believe it. All of it. I am incredibly good at my job." I frowned. "At both my jobs." I stretched up on my toes and kissed his cheek. "I love you, too, my darling. But this is something I have to do. And Snowy's life may depend upon it."

Eyes troubled, he slowly nodded. And then he got this silly grin on his face and began to laugh.

"What?" I asked.

"My wife, Regina I, Queen of Vesla, and Empress of the Golden Isles, is the most notorious outlaw in the Five Kingdoms! I don't know whether to be horrified or proud."

The western horizon was bleeding reds and gold into the sky, as Murdoch and I slipped out the postern gate, dressed in black and rid of those awful skirts for a while. I smiled at him. "Like old times."

Murdoch smiled his crooked grin. "That it is, my girl. That it is."

We moved from shadow to shadow in the better lighted areas of the city, crawling at times. The City Guard had changed from a fixed route to random years ago, at my suggestion. It was too easy to avoid them otherwise. Murdoch spotted a patrol just a block away in time for us to freeze in position with our heads down. They never saw us. I noticed that they were back to marching in unison and shook my head. I'd have to talk to Colonel Gebhart again – this time more forcefully.

The poorer areas had fewer lights and we slid through the darkness like sharks through the kelp forests. As we crossed Market, we heard Murdoch's name called. Turning we saw Fast Freda hurrying toward us.

"Murdoch! I'm so glad to see you, I heard some news... Oh, my God! Genie! It's you! It's so good to see you. Where have you been? I'd love to stop and chat, but..." She grabbed Murdoch's arm. "Slippery Steve heard from Gertie over on 8th and Fenmore that the 7 Dwarfs gang are meeting in the old factory, down by the river. You know, the abandoned one that's falling apart. They've been in and out of there a lot. And Gertie said someone spotted four of them carrying a package into the building last night. And the package was squirming and cursing something awful."

I reached out and grasped Freda's arm. "Thanks, Freda." and we hurried on.

Halfway to the factory, we were passing an alley, when a trash barrel rolled out in front of us and a tenor voice cried out "Stand and deliver!"

"Stand and deliver?" repeated Murdoch quizzically. "What the hell does that mean?"

The voice was a little hesitant this time. "It means you are to lay down your arms and toss your purses and jewelry to me." The voice broke on the last two words and squeaked up an octave.

I couldn't help it. I began to laugh. Murdoch joined in.

"You mustn't laugh!" the voice yelled at us. "This is serious."

I was still laughing when a very young man was rudely pulled onto the street by Murdoch. The boy was probably fifteen, tall and slender with blonde hair rather too long for my taste. He was ragged and filthy, with no shoes and a multitude of scratches on his face. At least he had a sword.

I stopped laughing. This boy had attempted to rob the Queen of Vesla. I regarded him with a steely gaze. "And you are?" I asked.

The boy drew himself up with remarkable dignity. "I am Prince Andrew George Reginald William Benjamin Alexander Wicksberg, Prince of Tavnia and son of King Gerald III."

I looked him over as he stood, ramrod straight, eyes fixed on the trash bins behind me. "A little down on your luck?"

His face was bright pink. "I was caught off guard by foul miscreants who stole my horse and shoes and left me to wander this horrid city alone. I managed to salvage my sword."

He looked down at the ground, a picture of misery now. "I wouldn't have hurt you, you know. I just need a horse and some things to get home."

"Does your father know where you are?" I asked.

Murdoch spoke up. "You ought to help him, Your Majesty."

The boy looked at me with a very cultured raised eyebrow. "You're a queen?" he asked, skepticism dripping from his voice. Since I was dressed in black shirt and pants, covered with dirt, with a sword at my hip, he might have been a bit incredulous.

"Actually yes. I'm Regina I of Vesla." I deliberately didn't introduce Murdoch.

The kid stared at me. "Really? Uh, I mean...An honor to meet you, Your Majesty." He bowed gracefully. I'm not sure he really believed me.

After we explained the situation and directed him to the castle, Andrew insisted on joining our tiny company. He wasn't about to miss an opportunity to rescue a princess. He swore he was a trained swordsman, so we took in this stray and continued to the factory.

Dark clouds had rolled in from the sea to the East, obscuring the stars. A light sprinkle wet our faces as we negotiated trash-filled alleys. Thunder rumbled overhead. The sprinkle turned to a shower, which had hopes of becoming a deluge.

Murdoch was leading as we approached the last corner. The three of us lined up, heads poking around the soot stained brick. The ancient factory building was outlined against the dark sky. Part of it had collapsed. The rest was missing most of its windows, giving the appearance of empty eye sockets in a skull. There was no light inside. Also no signs reading 'This way to the captive princess'.

A doorway, sans door, beckoned. We climbed the rock strewn slope to the building and peeked inside. It was dark. Very dark. Murdoch stood quietly with his eyes closed, listening and giving his sight a chance to adjust to the limited light. There was no sound except the dripping of water through leaks in the roof.

Murdoch waved his hand to the left and we headed down an aisle between rows of rusting and disintegrating machinery. They loomed like giant trolls to either side of us. I shuddered and almost ran into Murdoch when he stopped with his hand raised. He stood, turning his head, listening. I could hear something, too. A distant buzzing like bees in a hive. We headed in that direction.

Picking his way through the crumbling machines, Andrew banged his shin and almost, but not quite, throttled a curse. The buzzing noise grew louder, and eventually we could make out voices, several different ones, loud and angry.

Creeping along the aisle, we reached a wall. The voices came from the other side. Murdoch moved silently until he found a locked door. That was no problem for Murdoch. He had it open in less than a minute.

There was firelight on the other side, flickering around more deteriorating machinery. We slipped silently inside and squatted behind large engines. Words became audible.

"I say we slit her throat, dump her and get out of here." said a harsh male voice.

I smothered a gasp.

A deep rumble agreed.

Then the distinctive twang of Elizabeth's Waverly accent. "You will do nothing of the kind until I have taken the throne. She is far too valuable as a pawn." Muffled cursing followed that comment, and I knew my daughter was alive and well, if gagged.

"But, Your Grace, she's going to be a pain in the ass the whole time. She nearly gelded Grumpy here with that kick. She'd be so much nicer dead."

I grinned, whispering. "That's my girl."

Murdoch indicated with hand signals that I should stay put. He and the Prince slid silently along the wall from shadow to shadow, disappearing into the gloom. I knelt beside some boxes and peeked into the room. There were at least twenty dwarfs, sitting around a small fire. The Duchess was at an old desk in one corner, wearing a deep purple and gold cloak. She was working on something I couldn't see.

Snowy lay a few feet off, trussed up like a newly captured circus bear. She was gagged but seemed to be working on that; I could see her chewing on it. She was scanning the room when she focused on me. I grinned at her and gave a little finger wave. Her eyes widened and I thought she was going to choke on the gag.

Another voice spoke up. "If the King shows up with some of his guards, we're dead. Especially if she talks. Me – I'm getting out of here now. But first I'm going to shut her up permanently." A short, squat shadow rose from beside the fire and started moving toward Snowy.

The Duchess shrieked.

Almost simultaneously, Murdoch and Andrew jumped out from the darkness, swords flashing. I was a second behind.

Three were down before they realized what was going on. Then I was too busy fighting for my life to see much else. Murdoch appeared and we fought back to back. One dwarf was throwing daggers, pulling them out of his baggy pants. One flew past my nose and I heard Murdoch grunt. I slipped my own dagger out, and the dwarf threw no more. From the corner of my eye, I saw another dwarf, moving toward Andrew's back with a blade. My heart leaped to my throat and I screamed. But the small guy fell before he reached his target. Snowy had tripped him and now was beating him over the head with a wrench between her bound hands.

But there were too many of them. We were better swordsmen, but we weren't going to win this fight.

I saw Andrew cut Snowy's hands loose. He placed himself in front of her. Then I had three opponents and had no time for watching elsewhere.

It wasn't until one of my opponents lost his head – literally – that I realized reinforcements had arrived. Looking up, I saw my husband, wearing a purple and gold cloak, taking on the other two attackers. He dispatched them quickly.

"What the hell are you doing here?" I gasped.

He just grinned, as he parried another attack. I moved to cover his back and the next few

minutes were a blur of swords and blood and fear.

Then it was over. Four of the dwarfs were still on their feet, but Reynard's guards had them in hand. Elizabeth, however, seemed to have disappeared. Andrew had lifted Snow White up and placed her on a crate. He was carefully cutting off her bonds. I leaned against a motor and gasped for breath. Murdoch was breathing hard as well. He asked, "Are you all right?"

I choked out "Yes... Just...winded... Out...of...shape."

He nodded. "Also, getting older."

I glared. "Speak for yourself." I said, as I tied my scarf around the wound on his arm.

Snowy was going all gooey eyed over Andrew, who was fascinated by the cleavage she was flaunting.

Reynard had disappeared as well. I stood and looked around, going to the corner where I had last seen the Duchess. A syringe with a noxious green liquid inside lay on the desk. There were several apples lying around.

I thought I could hear voices. I found a door leading into the ruined section of the building. Rain dripped from the sky and from the broken masonry. A light flashed to my left and I started in that direction. I could hear the voices more clearly now: Reynard and Elizabeth.

"You will obey me." Elizabeth said in a voice, suffused with power.

Oh, my God, I thought. *She's a witch!*

"You will eat the apple." The voice repeated, a little more forcefully. "Eat the apple!"

I was maneuvering through the dark as fast as I could, scraping my legs on old motors. They were just up ahead. Dawn was breaking outside and I could just see them. Reynard was holding a bright red apple in his hand. Elizabeth stood twenty feet away, her right arm extended, handed curled with the index finger pointing at Reynard.

I screamed "No!"

Reynard glanced at me and tossed the apple over his shoulder.

Elizabeth shrieked in frustration and ran at him. I raced forward, but knew I wouldn't reach them in time. A knife rose up in Elizabeth's hand. As she attacked, a swirling of purple and gold enveloped Reynard. They came together and everything froze. For several long seconds they stood, face to face, gazes locked. Then Elizabeth staggered back, staring down at the hilt of Reynard's sword sticking out of her chest. The knife dropped from her hand, clattering on the cement. She slid to the floor. Her eyes looked up into the rain for a moment, then stared into eternity.

I stopped and stared at my sweet, gentle husband, who had just dispatched an evil witch.

He smiled. "You didn't really think I was going to eat that apple, did you?"

Snowy is still a teenager, and we still have memorable fights. But she is growing up. When she gives me sufficient information, she gets some privileges. I'm teaching her both armed and unarmed fighting, and she's very good at both. I haven't seen hide nor hair of Harold, Seymour's son, but Andy has made several trips from Tavnia to visit. He spends almost all his time with Snow White. Reynard and I are happy to see love blossoming between the two. And it won't hurt our relations with Tavnia a bit to join our two houses in marriage.

And as for me, I'm expecting our first child in a few months. Reynard is ecstatic. So is Snowy.

And so am I. I may name the baby Murdoch.

See Rhema Sayers's story "The Wicked Stepmother" online at Metaphorosis.
If you liked it, leave a comment. Authors love that!
Remember to subscribe to our e-mail updates so you'll know when new stories are posted. a comment

About the story

I love fairy tales and fantasy and always have. When I was a little girl, my favorite story was The Twelve Dancing Princesses. I always wanted to be a princess. When I got older, I wanted to be a queen. I had to settle for being boss of an ER for a 12 hour shift.

But my experiences in the ER, and the development of my personality over the years, have led me to value a strong, assertive woman with a wicked sense of humor.

It occurred to me that a story about a stepmother, dealing with Snow White as a horrible teenager, might be fun. Especially if the stepmother was a particularly independent and somewhat dangerous woman. From this beginning the character of Regina evolved.

A question for the author

Q: What five words describe you?

A: Curious, dedicated, assertive, risk-taking.

About the author

After 35 years as a doctor, first in Family Medicine, and then in Emergency Medicine, Rhema Sayers retired. She and her husband had adopted three little girls from China. Their daughters were all grown by the time she retired. So she turned to writing as a second career. It had been a passion when she was young.

In addition to writing, she loves hiking with her three dogs in the Arizona desert where they live and traveling with her husband, carrying a camera during both activities. Photography is another hobby.

She writes fiction, but also historical articles and stories based on her experiences in the ER.

The Draining

Matt Hornsby

It is strange to imagine that serpent-men might love serpents. After all, they go to great lengths to wreak destruction on the beasts, travelling far out on the fickle and changing sea to slay them. One might not imagine, too, that serpent-men love the Wetness. Yet they do. I never met a serpent-man who did not hold both the serpents and the sailing season quite dear in his heart. I surely loved both right well, in my own days at that trade. It is a strange kind of affection, one that was not owed simply to these things being my means of profit and promotion. It is a deeper bond, the tie that connects all creatures in struggle – the same as binds falcon and dove, wolf and deer. When, on a calm day, one spies a serpent breaching the black water, diamond-scales glittering on the massive curve of its back, it is a thing of great beauty; and as a ship bears down on it, harpooner scrambling to his post, one cannot feel a sadness that it will soon be dead, hide punctured and oil leaking across the timbers as it is hauled aboard. That, however, is the way of the world. It is the way that I followed myself, as a younger man, until that fateful voyage upon the *Whimbrel*, where all such things were cast into question.

The first Wetness had come early that year. I had watched from the boat-yard with joy as it filled the great mist-shrouded basin that stretched from the harbour to the horizon. The dark water rose higher every day, first submerging the clouds of fog, then then the tips of the highest reef, finally stopping at the lip of the port. What had been an empty void was a bountiful ocean.

For three seasons I had been sailing as a harpooner's boy aboard the *Whimbrel*, answering to Master Harpooner Mr. Lachlann Davison, conducting my duties with all due care and attention. This time I was sure that, with God's help, I would be rewarded with a chance to stand on the hunting-platform and claim a serpent as my own prize. Davison was a tough and quiet man, but he was honourable and generous to those who did good service; in that generosity he was quite unlike his own master, our notorious Captain Munro.

Yet once we had cast out onto the brimming sea, my hopes had been disappointed. Over that long season I had watched Davison take three of the creatures by his own hand. Before every kill, I hoped he might say that it was my turn to handle the iron; but every time he looked at me, he looked also to Captain Munro. Perhaps fearing the old man's wrath at a missed shot, he took all three himself.

"Watch and learn," he said, "and your time will come." I despaired. I had studied his craft for many months now, and with my eyes closed I could bring to my mind the way his legs braced against the swell, the way his eye followed his prey, the way his hand gripped the spear-shaft. I had watched and learned enough. I knew that I would disappoint neither him nor the Captain. The days were growing long, and I feared the pitying looks of my kinsmen and the wharf-girls should I return to the island still unblooded when the Draining came again.

I tested my fears on Bannatyne, the old Soundingman seated at the tiller, plunging-line grasped in his wrinkled hand.

"How many more days of Wetness?" I asked.

"We may hunt until St. Phadran's day, boy," he said, scowling.

"But it's already past Beltane," I said, my voice raw with disappointment. I had thought we would be out longer.

"You'll be lucky if we stay out that long," he said, with a cruel chuckle. "Munro's got three beasts already. Your Master Davison is onto his last harpoon. If the Captain's a wise man, he'll head back to port now, before the men get nervous of the Draining."

Sailors are fearful men, and serpent-men most of all. The sky's every shifting tone marks some dark omen or other: storms, scurvy, poor hunting, sharp reefs. Yet it is the Draining that they fear most of all, that time when the sea begins to sink, at first slowly, but quickening so that soon you can see it dropping with your own eyes. I had heard the old men say that in times past, before I was born, one could count the lambing-seasons and know the moods of women by the Draining, so regular was its coming; by the time of my childhood, however, the seasons had become uncertain. There was great tension and excitement as the Wetness drew to a close. As a boy, I had stood at the port and counted all the ships safely home, watching them dock and unload their cargo of scales and machine-oil. Occasionally, a ship would just miss the turning of the season and would need winching up to the docks from the sinking sea. Then, the beach became a clifftop as the water dropped away, eventually disappearing into a cloud of mist at the ocean-floor. Even from the safety of land, it was fearful to imagine what lay down below – perhaps the beasts of the depths, now crawling naked and hungry in the half-light, or perhaps nothing but a void, stretching from the cliffs to the world's end until the Wetness and the seas returned. There were a few men, old beggars on the wharf, who claimed they had been caught at sea when the Draining came and had seen the dried ocean-floor; but few put much stock in their addled ramblings. Many times more were the men who by the poor judgement of their captains had been caught in the Draining and were never seen again.

Sailing aboard the *Whimbrel*, I was not afraid of it. I was young, and I was sure that fate had marked me for success on this voyage. I felt a proud disdain for the miserable old Soundingman's caution, and I had trust in Captain Munro – a fierce and devilish man he might be, but there was no finer sailor and serpent-hunter. And I still trusted Davison, knowing that one day he would put his faith in me.

Davison must have read the disappointment my face after my words with the Bannatyne, for when I returned to my station on the hunting-deck, he fetched me a clap on the shoulder with his shovel of a hand.

"Season's not over yet, lad, and we've one iron left unbent," he said, laughing.

Then he seized my arm and leaned into my face, his breath salty and rich.

"I've taken a good haul for myself already," he said, casting a finger across the three serpents laid out on the deck, their scales glinting in the sea-mirrored light.

"If we spy a fourth serpent, here's my word – this strong arm of yours will be the one to cast the shot."

With that promise, I knew that before this season was out, I would take a serpent of my own or I would die in the attempt. I was the first on deck with every sunrise, straining my eyes at the horizon, searching the immense flatness of the sea for the beautiful arch of a serpent's back. Yet for all my efforts, nothing broke the surface bigger than a leaping water-wolf. As the days passed, I noticed a grumbling and muttering amongst the crew, directed towards the Captain. We had taken enough this season, they said. Port was calling, and Munro was still on a course out to sea, God take him.

Munro, for his part, stayed silent but for a few clipped orders. His most common station was on the hunting-deck, where we had hung the three great bodies of this season's serpents. At times he seemed to be admiring them and inspecting them for quality; at others he seemed to be guarding them, as if he feared that one of them might suddenly burst back into life and slither back into the ocean. From my position, I overheard my Master strike up words with him.

"Three beasts make a fine haul, Captain," said Davison as he swatted gulls from the serpent bodies with the tip of his harpoon. The Captain grunted in response.

"We'll get a worthy bounty," continued Davison. "The railway-men and metallurgists are offering a handsome purse for oil and scale. There'll be enough for every man to feed his family until the next Wetness."

There was a moment of silence. I fought back a desperate urge to tear my eyes from the horizon and look at them.

"Would you have me turn back to port, Mr. Davison?" said the Captain.

"With every day, the Draining draws closer. I would not bargain against the season, sir."

"You say that three beasts are enough. How much more adequate, then, would be four? We have one iron left to cast, and we

have our harpoon-master in fine health. I
say that we would be fools to return now."

Unable to resist, I turned the corner of
my eye to the two men. They stood facing
one another straight, arms across chests,
heads held proudly. For all that I
desperately wished he might, Davison
would not yield to the Captain. I did not
want to see him clapped in the hold; but
more than that, I wanted nothing more
than another two days sailing, so that I
might have my chance at a kill.

"Young Master Hardie is a man of my
own mind, I believe," said the Captain,
loud enough for me to hear. I snapped my
eyes back to sea at the mention of my
name. "Is that not so, Second Harpooner?"

I slowly turned my head to the two
men. Munro's single eye bored at me, as
black and cold as a cannonball. I knew
not how to answer without betraying one
of the men. In the end, Davison saved me.

"Back to your duties, Hardie," he said.
"We are still hunting."

On a warm, waveless morning, I mounted
the spying-deck and looked out to sea. My
heart climbed into my jaws. There, not

two leagues from us, was a black shape in the water, bigger than anything but a serpent. I began to raise the hunting cry, but the breath died in my mouth even as it gathered. The shape was not moving. I realised that I was looking at an outcrop of stone.

As my disappointment faded, dread crept into my fingers. We had not moved far since yesterday on account of the calm air, and I well knew there had been no rock in sight. I trod across the swaying deck to the Soundingman and roused him. When he saw the rock, the sneer on his old face melted into fear, and he frantically began to fling his plunging-line over the edge.

"We're dropping," said Bannatyne, his voice cracking. Davison spat a curse. Munro looked square at the Soundingman, his features unmoved.

"The Draining is not yet due," he said, "we have two more nights until St. Phadran's eve falls."

"I cannot account for the season, Captain, but I swear by God that the line and the gauge do not lie. We are dropping."

The Captain turned to the crew, gathered with their caps in hand.

"Turn the ship!" he roared, "Raise sail, and we will make port!"

"To the oars!" said Davison, steering me towards the rowing-benches. "Put that man's arm to use, lad."

For days I blistered my fingers as we pushed at the ocean. Fear drove my muscles. Two seasons ago, the *King Angus* had not returned home before the Draining. With the next Wetness, she had been found adrift, lifted again by the rising ocean, but with her crew either missing or half-eaten on the boat. None knew whether the eating had been done by whatever beasts might patrol the ocean floor or, in their hunger, by the crewmen themselves.

I turned my eyes to heaven and cursed God. We had not stayed out too long; the Draining had come early. Anger joined fear in my heart, and I drove it all into my rowing. Davison joined us, pushing his great oar through the water as easily as a child runs a stick through a puddle. The fear of that hellish seabed was in him, too.

But even with all our strength, we could not beat the changing season. Soon we saw whole ranges of limpet-studded peaks, encrusted with slippery sea-flowers and scuttling beasts, begin to push above the tide. Finally, as the reefs of Ard Manna reared before us, their corals and jagged rock blocking our way, the Captain bade us stop. We brought the *Whimbrel* to a halt, battening the hatches and fastening all gear to the deck. Then we sat and prayed, aloud now, until the water finally disappeared around us and we felt the ship's oak timbers crunch and sink into a tilted rest on the sand and rock.

The life of the sea – fish, serpents, crabs, worms and all – had vanished with the water, sucked into whatever realm could contain such a multitude of life. On the ocean floor, we were surrounded by desolation. In all directions stretched the great rolling plain of the seabed, as grey and bare as the sky above, broken only by the dark foothills of the reef before us. The plain was barren, home to nothing but a few bony corals and putrid weeds, little more edible than the sand in which they were rooted. Far overhead we heard the mocking cries of gulls and bonxies, safely beyond the range at which a man might fell one with a crossbow. The crew's eyes flickered towards the ration box.

We knew not what fate awaited us. The length of the Draining was uncertain. With our provisions, we could perhaps last eighty days marooned on the sea-floor; Munro's avarice had not seen fit to bring more supplies that that, and we had already cut into our store with a long season of hunting. We could do nothing but wait, hope and ask heaven for forgiveness, and that the Draining might by some miracle come early. I felt the faint rumbles of hunger begin to gather. The Wetness would return, or we would starve.

The days passed in fear. No man dared set foot outside the ship, into that unknowable wasteland of bleak sand and fog. The crew turned their backs to the *Whimbrel*'s keel, cowering against the beasts that they imagined without. I remained at my station. In the wind, I heard noises, and I scanned the mist, conjuring up lumbering shapes from every jutting stone and limp pile of kelp. We spoke little; every sound or movement brought pangs from my hungry bones, nights of torrid darkness and days of stinging salt wind. The men prayed, hanging their heads in silence, running their fingers over carved bone-charms.

From the butchering-deck the dead serpents taunted me. They could not fill our bellies – their flesh was poisonous as nightshade, food for machines rather than men. I hated myself for having cursed God; now I cursed my own greed and lust for honour. I had been desperate for Munro to keep sailing outward, keep hunting, even as all the other men desired to return. Perhaps I was responsible for this; perhaps God had seen fit to reward my childish ambition with a fitting punishment.

"Bannatyne", called Davison, breaking the low silence of a windless day, "how far to port, when the Draining came?"

The Soundingman rose his white-bearded head weakly. It had been forty days, and the old man was on the edge of death already.

"We're at the edge of the Ard Manna shoal," mumbled the Soundingman, "and nearly onto the Kelp Flats. Thirty leagues, or three days' sailing."

"Or two weeks' walking for a man with strength in his legs," said Davison, raising his voice.

There were murmurs amongst the crew. I imagined trudging across the blasted, horrible plain of the sea-floor, with neither shelter nor succour, at the mercy of whatever monster might rear up from a sandflat or coral shoal. Still, our desperation had grown. Such an end might be preferable to a slow starvation on the *Whimbrel*, in the midst of other desperately hungry men, and whilst we had heard rumours in the wind and mist, no beast had yet attacked us.

As the men's voices gathered, the Captain spoke.

"No man leaves this ship," he said, remaining at his station, legs planted firmly on the deck. "I will not abandon the serpents."

"You brought us on a bad voyage, Munro," said Davison. "Your hunger would starve us all."

I had never seen any man raise his voice to the Captain. He had an expression of minor annoyance, as if this rebellion were no more bothersome to him than a dry biscuit or a sharp morning wind.

"If any man leaves this ship, he will have no share in our prize. That is, if the sea-floor doesn't finish him first," he said. Then, turning to the men, addressing their rising spirits:

"The Wetness will return. God will not allow me to fail."

Davison jeered. "I would first put my life in the hands of the sea-floor than in yours. Damn you and damn your prizes."

I felt my heart twist at this. For a serpent-man to curse the ship's prize was for a mother to curse her daughter or a shepherd his sheep. It was not right.

"Men!" he shouted, "I am setting out on foot for port. With God's help, I will make it there in fifteen days, and I will take great delight in the company of any who join me." His eyes met mine as he said this, and there was the turning of a smile in his mouth.

My feet began to stir. I knew that he was calling to me to come, to tear myself away from the doomed ship. The other men were looking to me, I realised, waiting for me to take the first step; to give them licence to take a chance at saving themselves.

"Hardie," said the Captain. I froze at the sound of my name. "You will be the

First Harpooner of the *Whimbrel* now, with a First Harpooner's prize. You are worthy of it."

I trembled, taut as stretched wire, at this sudden promotion. I made to move off again, but I could not. A First Harpooner should not leave his prizes. The men knew that my loyalty had been conquered. The battle was over.

Davison left his remaining harpoon on the ship. He hoisted a bag over his shoulder and jumped overboard. He looked back at me, his smile gone. My eyes followed him where my feet could not, until he faded into the shimmering fog of the sea-plain.

I began to lose count of the days. As First Harpooner, I was afforded a greater ration: a crumb of dried biscuit and a swig of water. We ate in silence, hearing naught but the foul moaning of the wind across the seabed. The heat grew heavier, only interrupted by harsh winds that came loaded with fine, sharp sand that flayed the skin. When the wind stopped blowing, a stench would settle on us; the briny reek of wet sea-sand, blended with rotting seaweed. Our serpents added their own smell as they began to break down, oily and pungent. Laying on the deck between waking and sleep, I could not escape the staring of their giant glassy eyes. I thought of Davison, walking alone across the sea-plain, perhaps halfway back to port already, or perhaps already a meal for some giant and ravenous crab.

I tried to think of home: the flowing red hair of the girls, the purple blaze of heather in the hills, the rumble of the locomotive through the mountains. It all seemed lost in the greyness of the Draining, where there was nothing but coral and stone bleaching in the sun, gulls circling ever closer overhead.

It was the morning when something cold bit at my face in the darkness. At first, I did not respond. By then, I had little sense of time, and for days I had been in a state half of wakefulness, half of slumber. Yet the feeling was insistent of freshness and moistness on my face. I lifted a hand to it. It was cold. Bodies and voices were stirring across the deck. For minutes, I did not say anything, did not move. It was not just cold, but it was wet. Rain, coming in droplets ever thicker.

"The Wetness," I said. It was unreal, an impossibility, but others were doing the same, lifting their hands to their eyes in joy.

"The Wetness is here!"

I wept at the miracle; all of us wept, shaken in the joy of knowing that we would not perish amongst the corals and weeds. In that moment of elation, my fears fell away, and I felt nothing but the burning fire of life inside me. Our prayers had been answered, and the Wetness had come early, earlier than I had dared hope. After fifty days on the ocean-floor, we had been granted salvation. The prospect of hunger and slow death, which had stretched to the horizon in front of us, shrank away, and instead we saw only the gentle path home. The only man who stood unmoved was the Captain. In that moment he seemed to me like a savage, ancient god, unmoved by the petty travails of men and awesome in his power. He had been entirely vindicated.

"Lash up the rain-rigging," he called.

Within an hour, the ground beneath us had disappeared. We rose, the dark peaks of the mountains around us subsiding. We let the sails fly, and cast nets into the water, eager to catch the shoals that would accompany the rising sea. It was only after the smaller reef-spires had begun to disappear that I thought of Davison. Only ten days had passed since his departure from the boat. He had surely not had time enough. He would remain at the sea-bottom, beneath the water. Perhaps it was on him, I thought, that God's judgement had been visited.

His fate lingered on my mind, but it was tempered by the knowledge that I would live; the thought still seemed so strange and wonderful. Nothing ever tasted so sweet to me as the fresh foam on the air then, nor felt so comforting as the soft roll of the sea beneath us. Within two days sailing I would be on land, with silver in my pockets and hot meat in my mouth.

A shout came up from the forecastle.

"Beast in the water!"

I turned to the other men, unsure of myself, but now they looked to me for orders, as the First Harpooner. The Captain found his words first.

"Hunting stations!" he roared, spittle flying from his lips.

Munro had eaten the same poor rations as us when we were marooned; he had looked death in the eye as we all had. Yet even after that, he did not falter in his instinct to prove himself master of the sea.

I was almost too weak to lift the hunting iron, dragging it to my post at the bow. I had foreseen this moment so many times, imagined myself arching my arm gracefully back against the sails and hurling a mighty shot into an unlucky beast's flank. I moved my lips in prayer. The chance that I had lusted for was arrived. I would not miss it, even if I flung myself into the water with the force of the shot.

In the distance I saw the serpent, a black line against the calm sea. There was a strangeness to this one. A serpent's habit was usually to agitate, to dive at the sight of sails, putting distance between herself and men. This one seemed to float calm and still at the surface, as untroubled as an old man in his fishing-skiff.

As we drew closer, I saw a sight that turned my heart over. A tide of doubt, fear and wonder rose inside me.

In the water, there was a man. It was Davison. He was calling out in a small voice, paddling feebly at the sea. The serpent did not trouble him. Instead, it floated just beneath him, occasionally adjusting its position in the water to better spy us through curious red eyes, but always leaving one part of itself beneath Davison's tired legs. I could not fathom what its purpose might be.

The men threw ropes to him, beckoning and shouting at him to come aboard, but he did not move. I held the harpoon ready.

"I might have cursed you, Davison," shouted Munro, leaning over the prow, "but I will not let you drown. Come aboard."

Davison gathered his voice. It was thin against the sea-wind.

"Will you hunt this creature, Hardie?" he asked me. His face was twisted in pain. The serpent looked up at us. Up close and alive, the serpent was different from those that lay slain across our deck. The horned ridges and the barbed swords of its teeth were familiar; but the eyes, that in death were cold red stones, were burning and twitching around the world, looking at the boat, to me, to the gleaming iron in my hand. I could not but wonder how we might seem to it. As the creature bobbed gently below my Master as he struggled at the waves, I could find no other explanation than that it was attempting to keep him alive. Suddenly it was no longer a simple beast of prey, but a creature whose mysteries I had not come close to understanding.

"The beast showed me mercy," shouted Davison. "When the Wetness came, it lifted me above the water. I will not let you kill it. I owe it mercy," said Davison.

The Captain grunted.

"So be it. Your fate is your own, Mr. Davison. First Harpooner, cast when ready."

There was no questioning, nothing but clarity in his black eye, no suggestion of choice. I arched my arm, lifting the spear for a killing throw, winding what energy I had into it. But I could not let go. At that moment, when everything I had wanted was laid before me, I could not but push it away. My heart would not allow me to take it.

"I will not," I said.

"Then another man will!" roared the Captain. He looked hungrily from man to man. None came forward, nor raised his head.

"Then I will cast the damned shot!"

Munro advanced on me, hand outreached for the iron. My body moved before my mind did. I raised my arm again and threw the harpoon, line and all, into the dark sea. It had been our last. I had left the *Whimbrel* weaponless.

The Captain surveyed the crew again. No man met another man's eye, and yet we all knew each other's thoughts. There was silence, broken only by the low rumbling sound of the serpent's voice, shivering up through the wooden frame of the hull. The Captain seemed to shrink. In one second, he had held us to his will like captives; in another, he had broken the law that governs men's hearts, and in that moment, he had lost us.

He took his station, standing at the ship's stern, arms folded and long dark coat flapping around his ankles. No more commands came from his lips, and his power over us was gone.

We hauled Davison onto the deck. The serpent that had saved him slipped away into the lightless depth. None but God knows why it had shown him such kindness; perhaps even God himself sometimes finds mystery in his design. We sailed into port without much by way of word or deed. No man needed orders to do his duty and take us that far.

I know nothing now of those other men; not the old Soundingman, nor Davison with his arms of oak. I never more set to sea, but through all seasons, I stand on the hill and look out on the ocean; in the Wetness, I watch the serpents toss and tumble, red-eyed and dark in the distance, chased still by bobbing boats. And when the Draining comes, the wind blows in and drags at my ears – sagging now with age. In the sound of it I fancy I hear whispers, in that ancient language in which the laws of the Sea are written. I have long since stopped trying to understand them. It is enough for me to know that there are great mysteries in the hearts of men and the minds of beasts; riddles whose answers will never be solved.

See Matt Hornsby's story "The Draining" online at Metaphorosis.
If you liked it, leave a comment. Authors love that!
Remember to subscribe to our e-mail updates so you'll know when new stories are posted.

About the story

The story really came from a single, simple image — of a ship marooned on the ocean floor, with the ocean nowhere to be seen. It seemed like a powerful image of environmental catastrophe, and I added the idea of the ship being a hunting-ship, whose business is exploiting nature in the form of the 'serpents', to bring that element out. From there, the characters and the rest of the world just suggested themselves and developed iteratively. I've always been a fan of nautical narratives, and I enjoyed the process of creating salty sea-dog characters. In the end, what started as a very short story became a medium length one — the world and characters threw up a lot of questions, and I expanded the story considerably to try and answer them. Perhaps a shorter story would have been better, but I can never resist the world-building temptation.

The protagonist, Hardie, was initially quite a passive character, more of a viewpoint to narrate what happens aboard the ship than an actor himself. However, it quickly became clear that he was sitting awkwardly between the two positions, and decided to make him a fuller part of the story. I read back over some pre-twentieth century writing, particularly writing that features sailors, to try and get his voice right.

In any case, I hope people enjoy the story and take something away from it!

A question for the author

Q: If you could have a meal with a character from any classic novel, whom would you choose?

A: I recently read Ursula Le Guin's *Always Coming Home*, a book that is so comprehensive in its worldbuilding that it includes several recipes from the cuisine of the fictional Kesh, many of which sound quite appealing. So maybe I'd drop in on Stone Telling, who is the book's closest equivalent to a protagonist, for a bowl of valley succotash or acorn-meal soup with honey.

About the author

Matt Hornsby is based between London, United Kingdom, and Dublin, Ireland. When not writing, he works on environmental and economic policy, after previous lives as a scrap metal dealer and English teacher. "The Draining" in his second story in Metaphorosis, following "A Final Resting Place" in September 2019, and he has published other work in *StarshipSofa, Electric Spec*, and *Kzine*. Follow him on Twitter at @MatthOrnsby.

Sonata III: Canta

L. Chan

Adagio: Canta

This is the final part of L. Chan's novella, *Sonata*. Parts 1 and 2 ran in January and February 2020. What has gone before:

Sona, on a quest for vengeance, has enlisted help of the Six Named to play a piece of heretical Music composed by his mother, the Lady Kristyk. Shailani found Sona harbouring a second secret, a device of his mother's design, able to capture and replay any Music it hears, but the Music that Sona has brought is eerily familiar to her; containing elements of her own people's holy songs, Music she was sent up north to preserve. On their way out of the Six Named land, Sona's family, the House Deathsinger, caught up with them, and takes them back to the Capital under the watchful eye of Sona's half-sister, Canta Deathsinger.

Are you still unhappy about the Six Named? asked Canta. Sona did not answer. They were on deck, the other sailors keeping a respectful distance from their commanding officer. Canta sighed, fogging up her flying goggles from the inside of her helmet. This one smelt of stale grease and a stranger's sweat; Sona was still wearing her good helmet. Both she and Sona's guest wore airship spares. Her brother had his back to the railing, turning his head to the side to watch the farmlands and roads a mile below, the landscape spread like a drawn map. The winds nearly drowned out the sounds of the crew

I had no choice, brother. You did not lose five lives, you gained two. Father told me that I had to hunt down a traitor to House Deathsinger, a Six Named agent working against us, said Canta. *He trusted me above all others, because anybody else could be bought, but you can't buy me.*

She could see Sona's hands tighten on the railings, then relax and drop to his sides, ready. No expression there, and she couldn't read his eyes through the smoked lenses.

The Empire is sick, brother. The army bleeds the treasury; the only way it survives is through rapine and pillage. We can do better. Father has set our House on a trajectory upwards; we and our friends can take back power from the Emperor.

I wasn't suited for the army. I'm even less suited for your plots and subterfuge. I've been around the Empire since the Academy, Canta. Those that thirst for power are often ill suited to wield it. You'd do well to think about that, before you get caught up in something worse, said Sona.

It will be different, Canta said, hands growing more energetic. The world had seemed a much emptier place without her brother. Her father had begun taking her into his confidence when she started at the Central Academy, grand plans about taking down the rotten core of the Empire. Sona's death had ripped a hole in her, and what had come back didn't quite fill that space left in her soul. *You could help,* she said.

I'm not sure father has me in his plans anymore. He did send you to hunt down a traitor, did he not? asked Sona.

I'm sure he has his reasons. Empire factions have ears everywhere; best to keep it a secret, she said.

Even from you? asked Sona.

Even from me. The helmet stays on you at all times, whether or not my crew knows your face, she said.

How much longer to home? he asked.

Another week, perhaps, with a stop for supplies. Plenty of time to catch up, she said.

Maybe, he replied. *It's been a long time.*

It had, and Canta felt further from her brother than ever. *Do you remember when we used to race in the Skydock?* she asked.

They weren't races, I won most of them, he said.

I've beaten you before, Canta said, remembering the thrill of the chase and the wind rushing past her ears.

The week before your birthday? That was a gift.

It's not my birthday next week, brother.

We'll see if you've gone soft with the Capital, Cannie. When we get home, he said, and smiled for an instant, the brother she knew appearing for a heartbeat before he turned to face the wind.

The Skydock was the pride of the Capital. Spires of the palace might have been taller, but the flotilla of vessels at the dock, both military and civilian, was visible for miles around. The *Angelfall* had lines that distinguished her from the run of the mill brigantine, but Canta ordered her colours stowed and the ship berthed far from the Deathsinger piers anyway. Anything helped. The music carrying the brigantine aloft faded into silence, but the ship did not fall. All around them, audible even through the padded brass flying helmets they all wore, were the plodding tones of the Symphony of Industry.

The Skydock tower had an intricate system of organ pipes and whirling gears that ran a mechanical set of instruments, a horological marvel. The strong winds around the tower found their way through funnels and spun multitudinous windmills, flooding the entire Skydock with Sound, keeping all the vessels afloat in the air. Even the pull of the ground was lighter here. Canta could jump twice her height without even trying. Below, the Capital Sound covered the ground; from the grand palace in the north to the market quarter in the south. If she strained her eyes – and her eyesight was very good indeed – she could almost make out the Deathsinger manor on the edge of the Capital. People went about their business far beneath her, like so many ants. She sometimes wondered what it would be like to open up cannon fire from the Skydock, painting the streets below with hot iron projectiles. Holding people's lives in her hands, it felt very much like being a god.

Her crew got busy unloading her ship, coaxing her brother's multipede down the gangplank with some difficulty. He had always had a soft spot for those things. She sent the Far Islander ahead with her crew. Canta had business with her brother. She found him waiting for her at the bow, looking out at the hundreds of airships across the Skydock, bobbing with the ebb and flow of the deafening Symphony. He was wearing the spare helmet now.

We should get going, home is waiting, Sona said.

We haven't spoken in years, brother. There's never been anything we couldn't tell each other, Canta replied.

Everybody grows up.

Things used to be simpler. The world used to be smaller. We knew how we fit in it. I wish we could go back, Canta said, her sigh misting the inside of her goggles. *You said you wanted to see if the Capital had made me soft. Let's see if the Periphery's done the same to you. I need to know if my brother is still in there.* Canta pointed to the far end of the Skydock. The tower radiated piers like spokes on a wheel, with berths for paying customers. Other airships jostled for space, illegally lashed to each other to keep them from drifting away. The harbourmasters overlooked anything, for a price. Urchins and feral child gangs had a game; a footrace from one end of the flotilla to the other, making death-defying leaps bolstered by the same Sound that kept everything in the air. It was not foolproof, and a few children were lost every year. Lost but not missed. Not just the poor though; Sona and Canta used to run those races on days they were meant to be school in the science of Sound and the glorious history of the Empire. But their tutor had favoured strong drink at least one evening a week, preferring to set them reading dusty books and sleep away his hangovers.

The stakes? asked Sona.

Your story, if I win. The truth, she said.

And if I win?

Freedom.

I didn't know I was a prisoner, Cannie, Sona said.

Canta left that question in the air as she sprinted towards the stern of her ship. This was stupid. Beneath her. She had command of a ship, perhaps the best in House Deathsinger. A single misstep could cripple or kill her, the musical safety net notwithstanding. But here she was with the only person alive that really understood her. Time apart had thrown a wall up between them. Maybe she needed to go back to the beginning to see if they could ever be brother and sister again.

She imagined that Sona would be close behind. He had always been quick, but not as quick as her. Sona had indeed been the winner in most of their encounters, the competition equal parts a sprint and a puzzle of navigating the shortest route through moving airships.

The Capital opened up beneath her feet as she took a fifteen yard leap between two decks, the spread of ramshackle buildings a rot on the plains below. Her heart was pumping, sweat pooling inside the rough fabric of her flier's gear. She could see Sona catching up, his route diverging from hers. Canta was playing it safer, staying near the central spire of the Skydock, where the ships were densely packed, guaranteeing her next steps. Sona, on the other hand, was taking greater risks for a route which let him run at full speed, where the ships were less occupied and wider spread. His gambit was paying off. Canta was faster than she'd ever been, having spent most of her last few years amongst the clouds on ships like the *Angelfall*, and her footing on the bobbing decks was sure. Still, Sona had covered more ground than her, his tight frame allowing him to navigate the cluttered airship decks and swearing sailors.

Canta had a clear route to the finishing point, the end of the furthest pier from her ship. She put on a burst of speed, hoping to catch up with Sona. What she saw made her snort with laughter even as her breath dragged at her throat like a whetstone. Sona's gamble had failed him. As the ships grew sparser along his route, he was forced to make increasingly longer jumps. Until he skidded to a halt. A ship had launched, leaving a gap even beyond what his Sound enhanced bounds could cover. Landing in between ships was not without danger; the momentum of such a leap would surely punch him straight through the gentle lift of Sound carrying them all, and send him to his death below.

Canta pressed on, narrowing the gap. She was just about to catch up when Sona threw something from the ship he was trapped on. It looked to be a hatch cover he'd teased loose from the ship, flung in a mighty two-handed swing like a giant stone skipping across a lake. The wooden square spun slowly, buoyed in the air by Sound. Sona took a running jump, only managing half the distance between himself and the finishing line. Canta gasped as Sona hit the hatch and made a second jump, sending the wood to the ground below and pitching him to the finish line just before Canta crossed it.

Her brother was doubled over and wheezing with the effort, and Canta did not feel much better, collapsing in a heap at his feet.

What now? she asked, considering her options, wondering if Sona had kept up with his unarmed combat. Wondering if she could overpower him or if she even wanted to.

You've gotten faster, he said, pulling Canta to her feet, his grip firm. His journeys had not softened him, much the opposite.

Nice move. You could have died out there, she replied. *Your travels haven't made you any smarter.*

Spoken like the same girl who couldn't stand losing, said Sona. He paused, as though considering a dilemma of his own. Her brother drew a sheath of folded paper from his coat. Canta recognized his neat, compressed writing, filling each sheet from edge to edge.

Every month I was away, I wrote you a letter. It's all in here, he said.

You won, you know, she said, her Fingerspeech slowed by the numbness of her hands after the run.

Maybe, he said. *I've changed my mind about the prize. What I want is for you to trust me. Come on, it's been a long time since I was home.*

"So you've never been to the Capital?" asked Canta, while walking Shailani through the Deathsinger grounds. Sona had been holed up in the guest quarters since they arrived the day before and the Lord Antius was not expected back for some days yet, and she thought to get to know Sona's companion a little better. Unless Canta was mistaken, the ornaments holding up Shailani's braided hair were sharper than they had a right to be. Shailani had traded the Six Named outfit for clothes in the Empire style; not the court dresses, but the comfortable training clothes of Deathsinger initiates.

"I've never been this deep in the Empire." When the grey-haired woman spoke, her tones had the twang of the low counties. Army, then; all conscripts spoke that way.

"Deathsinger lands are on the outskirts of the Capital. We're far out because this used to be a fortified lookout, so the rooms are just shy of comfortable. It used to have its own spring, proof against any siege, even if the Capital has grown far beyond the old borders. Look," said Canta, pointing at mossy stone bricks overgrown with twisting vines and hairy nettles. "The spring has dried up, but the old aqueducts remain. Sona and I used to get into that one all the time. It leads all the way out of the grounds. One of the only exits that the guards don't know about."

"That's an odd thing to tell a guest, Lady Canta, let alone a prisoner. You're treating us well, but I have not seen or spoken to your brother since we arrived here. Nor have I been out without an escort."

"The Capital is a dangerous place, especially for members and guests of the Houses. My brother is unpredictable. When we docked, I thought I had him back, but he's retreated into himself since he's been here. My father is not a forgiving man. My brother may need your help getting out."

Canta forced those last words out; her father was not infallible, but she'd not doubted or defied him. Even this small betrayal took effort. The Lady Shailani was silent until they reached the fortress proper now. The night chill clung to the stones. Servants and singers alike bowed their heads when they passed Canta. She took care to acknowledge them with a nod or a smile as they went about their business. The other woman seemed unwilling to pursue the earlier conversation.

The Lady Shailani brushed the brass tubes snaking along the walls. "These look like those you have on airships," she said.

Canta nodded. "Speaking tubes, the latest in artifice for these grounds. Speak in one room, hear in another. Much better than anything you'll see down in the Far Isles. What is my brother to you, Lady Shailani?"

Lover? She didn't seem like Sona's type. If he even had one. Her brother was always so serious. Partner in crime? Perhaps. But what crime, exactly?

The older woman took slightly too long to answer. "Six of us were captured by Periphery brigands. Sona proposed a trade, my service as a translator for an opportunity for my five companions to escape."

"My brother fell in with brigands?"

"He was doing the accounts."

Canta allowed herself a small laugh. Her brother had always been good with numbers, one of the top students at the Western Academy. She had been better at the physical disciplines; even music theory was beyond her. She'd still been within the top three students at the Central Academy, at least in combat trials. Her father's choice of schools for his two children still puzzled her. Even with his impediment, Sona could have had the best pickings of the army or maybe in the government with one of the Maestri. Not within House Deathsinger, there was no place with one with his shortcoming in a choral House. Certainly not in the labyrinthine plots of the insurgency that her father had been plotting. Too much deference to authority in her brother. He'd never be a leader, but he'd be the best damn second in command anyone could ask for. Too much honour as well, but honour was only a cheap excuse for those unwilling to make hard choices.

The Lady Kristyk, now that woman had been a leader. Canta felt her loss even more keenly than she did her own mother's. Canta's mother had been high born as well, a distant relation to the Maestro of Order. Raised by governesses, she had taken the same dispassionate approach with Canta, fobbing the growing girl off to tutors or playmates. Not so the Lady Kristyk, and her two foreign born attendants (Canta had often heard Chun and Fong refer to the Lady Kristyk by her foreign name, but much preferred the refined tones of her Empire name). The Lady Kristyk had been more of a mother to Canta than her own; Canta's eventual success at the Central Academy had as much to do with the Lady Kristyk's foundational blade training as talent. She still kept a locket with the Lady's hair around her neck, thinking perhaps that she'd braid it into her own if she ever grew her hair out. Perhaps after she gave up flying.

The Lady Shailani gave up no more secrets on the rest of the tour, and the conversation tired Canta. She bid the other lady goodbye at the guest quarters, and nodded to the guards standing watch.

The Lord Deathsinger was due in hours. Sona remained closed to Canta, giving nothing and only asking for a single favour of her. A simple package for the Lady Shailani, but for what purpose he would not say. But first she needed to win the Lady Shailani over.

Canta led the Lady Shailani past the various studies, the sitting rooms, until they reached a small vestibule, lushly decorated in a bid to hide the practical and martial nature of the place. It had previously been the room where she and Sona took their studies before their academy training. Sometimes with tutors, other times with the Lady Kristyk. Canta fingered the abacus the Lady Kristyk had brought over from the Six Named land, eliciting glittering dust and the clack of stones within a wooden frame.

"Sona always did like his numbers. There's a small library in the next room. Would you believe Sona found one of the old passages there? A treatise on geometry hid a lever. Disappointment that the book wasn't real outweighed curiosity at the secret path."

"And you've delivered him to the one place he doesn't want to be."

Canta couldn't yet piece the two versions of her brother she saw. The one on the *Angelfall,* so eager to be back in the Deathsinger manor, and this reticent one that the Lady Shailani was describing. He'd always been the schemer between the two of them, the brains behind their joint mischief. His little sojourn had made him complicated, made his plans inscrutable. Again, she felt the keenness of the absence of the brother she remembered, as though he hadn't really returned and the glimpse of the old Sona at the Skydock had been a daydream. She needed to know more. Both about her brother and the outlander.

"Oh, Lady Shailani, only my brother's word kept me from leaving you with the Six Named to feed the carrion birds. He's home. He told me as much. Now, my House sent me to retrieve a traitor. I track him for half a year and it turns out to be my brother. I've not failed my House before, and I'm not about to start now. What I want to know is why my House branded him such and didn't tell me. Now, Far Islander."

"I think that's between you and your House isn't it? Your job is done. They say Sona's a traitor and your succession is clear, is that it? That's how you do it in the Empire?" asked the Far Isles woman, her soft slur all the more mocking, half twitch at the corner of her mouth. Canta felt pressure in her temples and behind her eyes, her left hand dropping to a sword hilt that wasn't there. She had to earn the Lady Shailani's trust, for her brother's sake, but she'd be damned if she'd let an outlander talk down to her.

"Look at you, wearing Empire clothes, flown over by the power of Empire music, living under Empire masonry. Shall I go further? Fighting in the Empire style, the civilization of your people an Empire gift. Your writing, your government. Empire gifts. That is how we do it in the Empire, we give."

The foreign woman was suddenly livid, not a raging forest fire, but a furnace fire. Not just one that could eat wood, but one that could melt steel. Yes, this Lady Shailani had killed before, of this Canta was sure.

"It's the contrary, Lady Canta. The Empire takes. Its hunger is endless. All the gifts you speak of, that's what Empire shits out after it eats the good in every place. Seribu would have found the good it needed in its own time," said Shailani, and her tone would have made the Lady Kristyk smile.

Seribu. Oh, the Far Isles. Names were confusing to Canta; the sciences and histories were Sona's area of expertise. She sighed. She was no closer to understanding Sona, and the Lord Deathsinger was due home soon. Canta worried for her brother. Her father was a complicated man, and shared little of his plans, even with Canta. She trusted her father, but she'd been sent up north to kill. Sona was too stubborn to take her help. So she needed a fallback. Sona needed a fallback. Shailani was all she had.

"Lady Shailani, you are here, in House Deathsinger. Things are in play. You are meeting my father in three hours. Sona has his own plan, but he needs someone to watch his back. What binds you to him?"

"Blood debt, for the five sisters he saved," said Shailani, but Canta discerned the split second of hesitation there. The Far Islander wanted something more, but as long as it kept Sona alive, Canta could not have cared less.

"Good. Sona wanted you to have this," Canta said, handing over the things her brother had given to her, sheets of music wrapped around what seemed to be a waxed cylinder, scored through with fine lines. Finding out her brother was still alive had been a ray of light for her, a promise of family, somebody that could look at her without weighing her usefulness to the cause of reforming the

Empire. Even her father saw her that way, a tool, unique in her loyalty because of her lineage, and all the more useful for the most delicate, the dirtiest work. She'd read through the music. It looked choral, but nothing like she'd ever seen before. Canta was complicit in Deathsinger plots, but the Houses plotted all the time. The secret histories whispered between the nobles said as much. But this, this new endeavour of Sona's was of a different order. Unsanctioned composing, heretical music. This undermined the very basis of the Empire. Still, Sona was her brother, and better his life than the Empire. She allowed herself her second smile of the day when it hit her that Sona would always be ahead of her; in succession, in the academy, and now, in treason and rebellion. Uncharted territory, but following Sona into trouble was blessedly familiar. Some things were impossible to grow out of, she supposed.

Canta escorted the pair to the audience room, where the Lord Antius Deathsinger held court. He was due back from the central Capital any time, and Canta had to ensure the audience was set up correctly. Sona had been sequestered in the guest quarters since he'd arrived, Canta seeing to his meals and needs herself. His requirements were blessedly small, a benefit from his travels. Nevertheless, the servants were already talking, and the secret could not be kept much longer. Sona walked beside her now, still in flier gear, with a servant behind him, bearing something Sona wanted to present to father, some complicated contraption with gears as small as those of clocks, moving spindles, and the like.

The audience room was ornately decorated, fashioned after the more opulent trappings of the Maestri, but only superficially so. The furs here were more common, the tapestries less vibrant, the silks more coarse. Father saved the Deathsinger purse for the cause. The chamber was guarded by Deathsingers, outside and within. Six inside, each a product of ten years of hard training, able to kill with voice, weapon, or empty hands.

Lord Antius entered the room behind them, making his way past the guards, down the length of the room, past the waiting trio and Sona's assembled device. He took his seat at one of a pair of large, carved chairs at the head of the room. Far Isles wood, dark as blood under the moonlight, harder than the jaws of termites. The other chair was empty, and had been so since the death of the Lady Kristyk. Canta smiled at her father, who did not smile back. She could see herself in him, but not in Sona. Tall and severe, hair turning to grey at the temples, Lord Antius was thinner than he used to be, but imposing nevertheless. These days, he subsisted less on sleep and food than on his machinations with his conspirators, but he had never had more energy.

Sona, he said, *you can take that off. I knew your sister didn't have it in her to kill you.*

The flier helmet hit the ground. Canta always wondered, as she did again, about the potency of Six Named blood, so different did her father and brother look.

Father, said Sona, his Fingerspeech slow and deliberate, *are you sure you want to have this conversation in front of Canta and your attendants?*

She can stay. She deserves to know and to be tested by knowledge. How else will she build a new Empire? asked Antius.

Was the Western Academy a test? The murder of your wife? asked Sona, taking a step forward. Antius held up a hand. The guards stopped, the fastest of them already past Canta. What was Sona accusing her father of? Sona had claimed Empire involvement in the razing of the Western Academy, but there were children of all Houses there. Of all the Houses, the double tragedy that befell House Deathsinger at the massacre put them the furthest from suspicion. Or so she'd believed.

The Lord Antius signed to Sona, but his gaze was on Canta. *Another test, everything was a test. The ascendancy of our House was not easily won. Power comes with position, and with continuity. Continuity of blood. House Deathsinger would not have the support of the older Houses if the mantle would one day pass to you, Sona. Your mother was a remarkable woman, even if the Six Named streak in her was never tamed. Few things keep me awake at night. Your mother's death is one of them,* he said.

Canta felt the same vertigo, the same ground sickness she felt after a long flight, as though the flat earth itself were rolling and yawing. Sona's expression had relaxed, as though a weight had been lifted from him. Shailani on the other hand, wore something much more inscrutable, a small frown of confusion.

Sona had reached his device. Canta had checked it herself. No blades, no darts, no poisons. Nothing capable of touching the Sound either; no bells, no strings. What was that thing?

Not as mother spoke to me, Antius. No Fingerspeech. I want to hear you say it, said Sona.

"Sona, we need not go through this. I loved your mother. I have no enmity towards you. Your death would have been quick, under the guise of a larger raid, to be blamed on separatists and insurgents. House Deathsinger would be inherited by Canta, Empire blooded and highborn," said Antius. His voice, unlike his body, had not withered and possessed the same low baritone that he could use to crush rock or pulp bone.

"Your own son?" asked Canta, drawing all eyes around the room.

"Honour is only for those that are too weak to make the hard choices, girl. The future of the Empire and of the House is paramount. I did this for you. What I do next, I do for you."

Hold, Lord Antius, a trade for my freedom and that of my companion, said Sona. *The Lady Han sent me to complete her work, work that she only fed you crumbs of. You believed, against the catechism of the Empire Sound, that music could be trapped, and replayed. This is the player. The recorder will be sent to you when our freedom is assured, and you will never see me or Shailani again.*

The Lord of House Deathsinger drew himself to his full height and advanced on his remaining kin. "So, she finally completed it. You needed me to speak and not use Fingerspeech because your machine both traps and releases Sound. You would have made a better Lord Deathsinger, I think, but betrayal is a skill that you've not practiced." He nodded to the guards, who drew their weapons, clucked to clear their throats to deploy Sound.

In a heartbeat, Sona and his companion would be dead. Canta just hoped, as she lobbed the pair of double-walled glass ampoules at the ground between them, the volatile mix igniting and producing acrid smoke, that the Far

Islander was worth whatever she was being paid. The opening bars of the guards' deadly songs turned into coughs and choking sounds. Quicker on the uptake than most, the Lady Shailani covered her mouth with a sleeve to filter out the smoke. She had already drawn out a black cylinder from the contraption, swapping it for another from about her person. Was that the one that Canta had passed to her? Sona had already liberated a sword from one of the coughing guards, despatching the guard with quick cuts to the hamstring and shoulder, turning to face those recovering from their convulsions.

Canta met the eyes of her father, looking down at her over steepled fingers. Sona was good, but not good enough for these odds. Her hand rested on the hilt of her short sword. The weapon was the perfect length for fights on airships, short enough to swing in the tight corridors and decks without snagging, but here the guards had the advantage in arms. She'd already sealed her fate when she smoked out the singers. Wetting her blade was just an afterthought. The Lord Deathsinger already knew what she was going to do, and he looked away. He had tested Canta, and she had failed. Of the two Sonas she brought back from the Six Named land, this was the true one. The one that the Lady Shailani saw, the one that was going to betray House Deathsinger. Her father had told her the truth – she had brought back a traitor. But still she could not let her brother die. She drew her sword just as the music started.

Canta had never heard its like before, and part of her academy training had been the study of all four major Symphonies and the minor pieces that made up Empire canon. This was something completely new, and that meant a Composer outside of the Empire's control. What heresy had her brother wrought? His device was clever, but this? A new composition, outside of the will of the Emperor? That chipped away at the very foundations of the Empire. There was a reminder in the very naming of the Empire Sound – that the Empire drew its power from Sound and that all Sound belonged to the Empire. The music itself had a numbing effect, the air itself vibrating. It reminded her of the times she had taken her airship over deserts or the sea, and seen the mixing of layers of air, the flow warping and distorting the view of everything in beyond it. Guardsmen and women were coughing, still trying to clear their throats of acrid smoke. Canta gave one last look at her father and stepped forward to defend her brother. That was when the Far Islander began to sing.

The words were less familiar than the tune. They must have been in Shailani's own tongue. Canta's blade dripped. The heretical music grew in volume and in effect; she felt the power of it in her bones. The ebb and flow of combat threw her beside her brother. She looked into his face for the slightest sign of guilt, of any regret for bringing this monstrosity into their home. There was nothing there, nothing but the concentration of a man fighting, not desperately, but with little more passion than he'd put into sword drills. He'd planned this. Maybe not the sequence, but that here, in front of their father, he would unleash something dark and forbidden. Canta wanted to scream, to turn her blade against her brother, to deploy her own Sound against her blood. Nothing came out. That was when Canta saw her.

Indistinct at first, a heat mirage of a woman. The outline fleeting and wavering at first, but her form emerging, as though she were stepping out from a fog. A woman made out of the same distorted light that the Sound was blanketing the room in, visible in form the same way an eddy or a whirlpool was visible, composed of fluid but given shape, and that shape was of the Lady Kristyk. Her approach stilled the fighting, as both the guards and Sona stared at the woman made out of Sound.

The Lord Deathsinger was on his feet, and there should have been fear on his face, as there was on the faces of all the guards, unsure of whether to advance in the face of this strange and perverted Sound. Instead there was something serene in his visage, something Canta had not seen before.

"I'm sorry," said the Lord Deathsinger to the apparition. And it was a day for firsts, because Canta had not heard those words pass his lips all her life.

And the woman made of Sound spoke, and when she spoke it was with the foreign words of the Far Islander, it was with the crash of the musical instruments of the land of her birth; the clang of metal, the wail of strings, the blaring of trumpets. She looked at the Lord

Deathsinger, engineer of her kidnapping and her captivity, and she said that she forgave him. She leaned in to kiss him on the lips, and when she drew back, the man was dead on his feet, a single tear of blood welling up from one eye and rolling down his cheek, a trail of crimson against his white skin.

Sona was up beside his father, rushing past him, not to catch the collapsing man but to activate the speaking tubes to the rest of the fortress. His face was twisted at the sight of his mother, as though he had not expected the music to call her back. The Far Islander, Shailani, was clawing at her throat, the words coming out ragged but still drawn from her involuntarily, as though the music sat unhappily on her stomach and was only now coming forth in a continuous stream of bile and lyrics. Canta still had her sword in her hands, and she took a step towards her brother.

The Lady Kristyk was less kind to the guards; her touch was gentle but the effects were not. Bone folded in on bone, the snaps like cannon fire in the enclosed space, white shards erupting from liveried uniforms. Then there were four in the room, the traitor, the singing foreigner, the angry ghost of a woman she would have once called mother. And her, heir to House Deathsinger. Outside, the screams were just starting.

Her death stalked her, through the swirling dregs of the smoke on the floor, around the corpses of the guards. The Lady Kristyk, with murder in her eyes and killing in her touch, gaining on her. Soon she'd be cornered, the same fate for her as for her father and the guards. She faced her reckoning on her feet, back to a wall and with her sword ready. Until Sona put himself between her and his mother.

He said something, something that she couldn't see from behind him. The Lady Kristyk was not to be appeased, halving the distance between her and him in a single surge. She was nearly upon him when the crash of wood and metal onto the ground brought the music to an end. The apparition vanished.

Sona spun around, palms up and open, weaponless.

This was not what I wanted. I can explain, he said.

House Deathsinger in ruins; the dream of reform dead and cooling on flagstones like her father. The entire conspiracy, headless and lost, until the Empire's spymasters closed in, putting them each under question and torture.

"No," said Canta, finally finding her voice, remembering her brother's hand on the speaking tubes. "It's exactly what you wanted." She stepped forward and put her sword in his gut. Another second more and she would have twisted her blade, spilling his bowels out onto the floor, to join her father's blood and her own tears.

Was she crying for the father taken from her or the brother she had lost?

Sona looked away, unwilling to meet her gaze as she killed him. No matter. She tensed, ready to finish it. Shailani hit her from the side, coming in quick from her blind spot. That woman knew how to fight, her first kick a heeled stomp to the side of Canta's leg. Something in her knee gave way. But Canta didn't need weapons to kill, her voice had always been her most potent weapon.

She was still inhaling when the knife edge of Shailani's hand struck her in the throat.

Codetta: Sona refrain

The chills woke Sona up, his fevered body soaked with sweat. His torso would not obey him. Under the blanket, he found bandages, damp with sweat and sticky with blood. A hunched man was nearby, wringing out a damp cloth into a metallic tray. Shailani was beside the bed, dozing while slumped backwards on a chair. The man laid the cloth on Sona's brow and shook the woman.

Shailani sniffed, cleared her throat and spat on the floor. The man grimaced.

"You're awake," she said, her voice still ragged from the strain of the Lady Han's song.

Where are we? he asked, signing with one hand while the other pressed down on his stomach. The pain was coming in waves now.

"Old military network, hospital for pensioners and veterans. Very discreet for those who've served," Shailani said, showing Sona the colours of the Sixty-Seventh she had tattooed over her forearm.

How did we get out? asked Sona.

"Your sister had a plan, a failsafe. She showed me a way out. Of course, she didn't expect to stick you through the belly first. Wasn't a need to sneak out after your Music had done its job. Thank the spirits for that multipede of yours; I don't think I could have hauled your ass out of that forsaken fortress."

Sona lay back on his hard pallet, the muscles in his middle complaining and aching.

I didn't think that was what the music would do, he said. When he closed his eyes, Sona could see a woman made out of Sound tearing through the guards, parting flesh like so much wet paper. He did not want to remember his mother like that.

"You had some idea after the festival."

Sona folded his arms, remaining silent. He had, of course. The Empire had reduced the Sound to its martial components but there was more to it than any Empire Composer understood. The Lady Han had not grown up within the Empire canon. She had other ideas, melding the baser musics of her homeland into an Empire symphony, and touching parts of the Sound that had never been delved before.

Did anyone see us flee? he asked, not ready to discuss his mother's music.

Shailani stretched, arching her back like a cat. "I honestly didn't have time to check, being busy with running for my life and you leaking blood all over me." She paused. "Probably. They'll be questioning those left alive."

Canta? he asked.

"Alive, probably. I didn't kill her. Spirits knew she deserved it for what she did in the Six Named land. She was dear to you, though."

I thank you for sparing her, although she'll make us regret it someday.

"Empire's a big place. Hell, so's the Capital."

Canta can be very single minded. She found me once, after all. Not just her. My father had allies here. Friends in the shadows. The Capital is a dangerous place for us now. Thank you for saving me, said Sona, turning his head to look at Shailani. *It gets muddled after she stabbed me. What happened to the device?*

"Destroyed. Though it took more strength than you know for me to have done it. We could have used that to save the dying language of my people."

So those were the words you sang, said Sona.

"Your Music, my words. It's something... sacred to my people. The Six Named recognized it as well. When Canta gave me the music, I was sure. It's the same music my sisters were trained in, something to ease the passing of the dead from this world to the next."

We wouldn't have gotten out without it, Sona said, and snorted. *So I've won, I've thought long about bringing justice to my father, and now that the House has fallen. All it cost me was my sister. Maybe my father and I are not so different after all.*

Shailani put her hand on his arm. "You fought your own war. We all carry something out."

Even retired sergeants? asked Sona.

"Even us. Where to for you?"

I've been on the move so long, nowhere feels like home. I can't stay here. The Six Named land will not have me. Maybe Pendulos. There's still my mother's research there, things I can do. Her plan for me was never revenge, or to follow in her work. She was uncovering things forgotten by the Empire, in the music she was writing. Something you helped me see when you completed her Music. Or the devices she had people working on, like the piece I brought here. It would be nice to build something again.

"You're always running away to tinker with things. I once asked you if you wanted to change the world, and you opted for vengeance. Even your sister believed in building a better world."

Sona paused. Of the sacrifices he thought he would have to make on his quest, he had never considered his sister. He'd taken everything from her, and all while she trusted him.

Revenge has already cost me the only family I had left, he said. He could not meet Shailani's eyes and his hands were shaking. *But I did what I had to, right?*

"Good. You're growing up. And do you harbour your family's ambitions?" asked Shailani.

I'm not like Cannie, thinking that I can save the Empire, or jostling for power with the other houses. I'm a child of the Empire, but I'm done growing in its shadow. I'll never be Six Named. I'm not going to be Empire. I'll find my own way, answered Sona, and that seemed to satisfy Shailani.

She left the room and a familiar tinkling tune followed her back in. Sona was pleased to see the multipede again. He'd grown attached to the thing and missed the banal little ditty that kept him company up the Periphery.

"You say you're not Empire, but you still put yourself at the centre of the world. There's nothing more Empire than that. Do you realise you've not spared a word to ask about me since you woke up?"

The last words were spoken loud enough to bring the attendant from the next room. Shailani waved the man away. Sona was unaccustomed to guilt, or perhaps his heart only had room for the guilt of letting his mother save him. He wouldn't have finished his own journey without Shailani. Each of her words felt like a blow.

Sona winced as he swung his feet off the bed onto the floor. It'd be some time before he healed. Shailani'd repaid her blood debt many times over. More than that, she was the closest he'd come to having a friend since he started his journey.

It has been a long road for me, Shailani. It has been difficult to trust anyone since the Academy. You've done more than I asked at the Periphery, and asked for nothing in return. You're even further from your goal than when we started, he said.

Shailani was still for a moment, the room silent, as though everything held its breath for her answer. "I was bound by honour for a while, but we only agreed

that I'd help until you left the Six Named."
She looked up. "For a while, I was hoping
to steal your machine, bring it back home
for my people. Maybe I just wanted to see
you beat the Empire, or at least a little
corner of it," she replied.

Thank you for getting me here. It's
been a long time since I've had a friend,
he said.

"I can't stay in the Capital. Like you
said, I'm further away from the other
Keepers than I ever was."

*Pendulos is too warm for my liking at
this time of the year. You might need
someone who's been around the north,* he
said. Shailani smiled, and it was a rare
thing to see her face crease up with joy.

"You needed bandits as tour guides."

You were kidnapped by peasants, he
said.

Shailani offered him a hand and helped
him to his feet. "To the north?"

North it is.

*See L. Chan's story "Sonata III: Canta" online
at Metaphorosis.
If you liked it, leave a comment. Authors love
that!*

Remember to subscribe to our e-mail updates so you'll know when new stories are posted.

About the story

"Sonata" is one of the longest things that I've written (and completed). I don't often work in the fantasy sandbox, I much prefer near future science fiction and contemporary fantasy. For "Sonata", what preceded the story was the world building — a magic system that fell roughly as another aspect of the physical world, and where the control of that magic ran along political and societal faultlines rather than through resource or genealogical lines. Things flowed on from there — an extant Empire with a colonialist reach, a good old fashion revenge quest and some non-traditional characters. It didn't get really steampunky until about halfway in, when I realised that the frame of having a sound based magic system would overcome a lot of the engineering limitations of steampunk without pushing the rest of the technology of the world into the industrial revolution or thereabouts. It was also important to me to retain a tight cast of characters this time round, although the roster is definitely going up if I ever return to these folks.

A question for the author

Q: What inspires you?

A: Many things! I'm the filter feeder in the inspiration food chain. Sometimes, it's bouncing ideas off tweets with friends. Sometimes I start with a title but no story. Sometimes I start with a line or a scene with no idea how the rest of the story goes. Recently, I've tried to address some weird imbalances in tropes that irked me, like the Selkie myth.

About the author

L. Chan hails from Singapore. He spends most of his time wrangling two dogs. His work has appeared in places like *Translunar Travellers Lounge, Podcastle,* and *the Dark*. He tweets occasionally @lchanwrites.

lchanwrites.wordpress.com

Copyright

Metaphorosis Publishing

Metaphorosis offers beautifully written science fiction and fantasy. Our imprints include:

Metaphorosis Magazine
plant based press
Metaphorosis Books
Driftwyrd
Vestige

Help keep Metaphorosis running at
Patreon.com/metaphorosis

See more about some of our books on the following pages.

Metaphorosis Magazine

Metaphorosis
a magazine of speculative fiction

Metaphorosis is an online speculative fiction magazine dedicated to quality writing. We publish an original story every week, along with author bios, interviews, and notes on story origins. Come and see us online at magazine.Metaphorosis.com

Keep Metaphorosis running! Support us at
Patreon.com/metaphorosis

You can also find us at:
Twitter: @MetaphorosisMag, @MetaphorosisRev, @Metaphorosis
Facebook:
www.facebook.com/metaphorosis

We publish monthly print and e-book issues, as well as yearly Best of and Complete anthologies.

Metaphorosis: Best of 2019

The best science fiction and fantasy stories from *Metaphorosis* magazine's fourth year.

Metaphorosis 2019

All the stories from *Metaphorosis* magazine's fourth year. Fifty-two great SFF stories.

Metaphorosis:
Best of 2018

The best science fiction and fantasy stories from *Metaphorosis* magazine's third year.

Metaphorosis
2018

All the stories from *Metaphorosis* magazine's third year. Fifty-two great SFF stories.

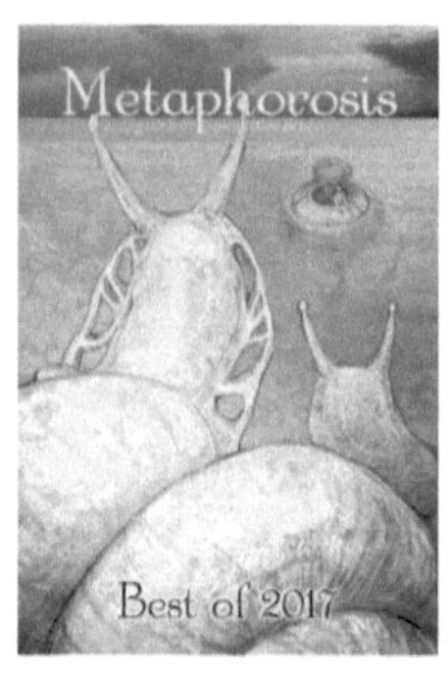

Metaphorosis:
Best of 2017

The best science fiction and fantasy stories from *Metaphorosis* magazine's *second* year.

Metaphorosis
2017

All the stories from *Metaphorosis* magazine's second year. Fifty-three great SFF stories.

Metaphorosis:
Best of 2016

The best science fiction and fantasy stories from *Metaphorosis* magazine's first year.

Metaphorosis
2016

Almost all the stories from *Metaphorosis* magazine's first year.

Plant Based Press

Vegan-friendly science fiction and fantasy, including an annual anthology of the year's best SFF stories.

Best Vegan SFF of 2019

The best vegan-friendly science fiction and fantasy stories of 2019!

Best Vegan SFF of 2018

The best vegan-friendly science fiction and fantasy stories of 2018!

Best Vegan SFF of 2017

The best vegan-friendly science fiction and fantasy stories of 2017!

Best Vegan SFF of 2016

The best vegan-friendly science fiction and fantasy stories of 2016!

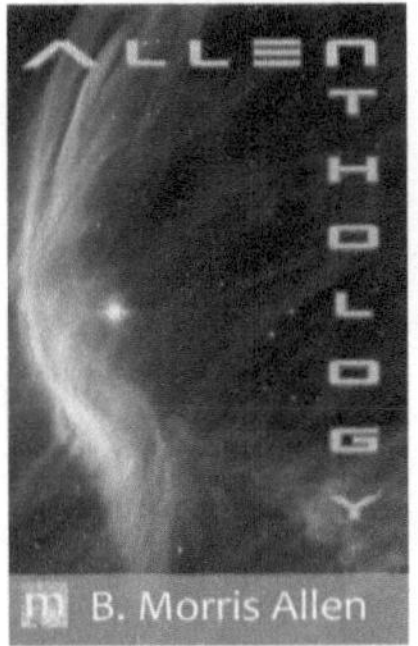

Susurrus

A darkly romantic story of magic, love, and suffering.

Allenthology: Volume I

A quarter century of SFF, including the full contents of the collections *Tocsin, Start with Stones,* and *Metaphorosis.*

Metaphorosis Books

Science fiction and fantasy books for writers – full of great stories, often with an additional focus on the craft of speculative fiction writing.

Score

an SFF symphony

What if stories were written like music? *Score* is an anthology of varied stories arranged to follow an emotional score from the heights of joy to the depths of despair – but always with a little hope shining through.

Reading 5X5

Five stories, five times

Twenty-five SFF authors, five base stories, five versions of each – see how different writers take on the same material, with stories in contemporary and high fantasy, soft and hard SF, and a mysterious 'other' category.

Reading 5X5

Writers' Edition

All the stories from the regular, readers' edition, plus two extra stories, the story seed, and authors' notes on writing. Over 100 pages of additional material specifically aimed at writers.

9 781640 761667